REA

FRIENDS

APR 2 2005

OCT 1 6 2004

HIGHLINE RIDERS

Other books by Howard Pelham:

Death Canyon

HIGHLINE RIDERS

•

Howard Pelham

AVALON BOOKS
NEW YORK

© Copyright 2004 by Howard Pelham
Library of Congress Catalog Card Number: 2003097363
ISBN 0-8034-9651-6
All rights reserved.
All the characters in this book are fictitious,
and any resemblance to actual persons,
living or dead, is purely coincidental.
Published by Thomas Bouregy & Co., Inc.
160 Madison Avenue, New York, NY 10016

.

PRINTED IN THE UNITED STATES OF AMERICA
ON ACID-FREE PAPER
BY HADDON CRAFTSMEN, BLOOMSBURG, PENNSYLVANIA

I would like to express my thanks to Mira S. Park and the editors at Avalon Books for their helfpul suggestions in the writing of *Highline Riders*.

Prologue

New Mexico Territory
Summer, 1865.

The small wagon train, nine wagons in all, rolled across the New Mexico prairie, leaving behind a cloud of dust which, though undersized, could still be seen for miles across the level, rolling land. No one in the wagon train spotted the lone Kiowa warrior who sat on a spotted pony on the flat mesa two miles away.

The Kiowa studied the wagon train a moment longer, turned his mount about, and rode toward a trail which led down from the mesa. He joined a party of twenty-five warriors who waited, hidden from view behind the mesa. The warrior conferred with his brothers for a few moments.

Then, leading the party of warriors from behind the mesa, he gave a high-pitched yelp, held his rifle above his head, and kicked the spotted pony into a gallop toward the wagon train. Behind him, rifles held high, the party of warriors followed, their chorus of yelps raising a frightening din.

The Indians closed in before the wagons could circle. Jumping from their mounts, they took the settlers on in hand-to-hand combat. Though a few of the Indians went down, the settlers were outnumbered. Ten minutes later, not a settler was left alive. Not even a child had been spared. After gathering up all the weapons they could find, the Indians looted the wagons and set them on fire. Tying their plunder on the backs of the horses that had pulled the wagons, they fled away across the terrain, past the mesa, and out of sight.

An hour later, two riders approached the mesa from the opposite direction. One was a man, maybe fifty, the other a boy of fourteen. When they sighted the remains of the wagons, the boy kneed his horse and sent him toward the wreckage in a fast gallop.

"Hold up there, boy!" the man yelled. "You may be riding smack dab into a hornet's nest!"

The boy pulled up and waited for the man to catch up.

"Now let's ride in there with some caution," the man said.

As they neared the wagons, smoke still trailed up from a few, but nothing moved. The boy found his parents' wagon and stared down at their bodies. "They're both dead," he said to the man beside him. "How soon can we go after them Indians, Rusty?"

"What good would it do?" the man asked. "Your folks are dead, and going after their killers won't bring them back. We'd be outnumbered and in a strange country, a country them Indians know well. We could get ourselves killed just as dead as Tobin and your ma. Think now. Would they want you to throw your life away?"

"No," the boy said after a moment.

His shoulders suddenly slumped and sobs wracked his body. The man put a hand on his shoulders. "We'll bury them, Jason," he said. "Then we better hightail it out of here before some of them rascals come back."

Chapter One

Arizona Territory
Summer, 1878.

The Arizona sun was hot on his back when Jason Ward rode into the valley and looked down on a broad expanse of grass and trees that some ranchers might have killed for. This was the second time he'd looked on this valley which he now owned. He had wandered into the valley earlier, looking for unclaimed government land to file on. Then he had ridden into New Castle, filed, and returned for another look.

Again he admired the site. Tall mountains surrounded several square miles of grass belly-deep to a horse, and a nice stream cut through the valley. Trees, mostly cottonwood and willow, grew along its banks, providing plenty of shade. A perfect place to raise cattle, Jason said to himself, and thought of the mostly dry and dusty ranch he and his friend Rusty Hayes presently owned in New Mexico.

Jason was sure Rusty would like this land, and then they

could sell the ranch near Cimarron and use the money to help stock this place.

Jason was of medium height but solidly built, broad across the shoulders and slim of waist and hips. Thick, slightly curling blond hair showed beneath his flat-crowed, flat-brimmed hat. Brows a bit darker than his hair hovered over blue-gray eyes that stared from a face burned dark by the sun. The nose was straight, the lips thin and firm, and the solid jaw lent strength to the features.

With a smile of pleasure at the sight, Jason watched a small herd of antelope rise from where they were bedded beneath some trees, stretching as they walked to the stream for a drink. A few more, wading through the deep grass, straggled to the shade, stopping occasionally to pull at the graze.

Jason rode a big sorrel, his favorite mount. The horse had staying power and was fast but Jason liked him more for his uncommon gentleness. It's rare for a horse not to jump when one shoots a gun from his back, but Jason had trained the sorrel well. Now the animal stood unflinching when a gun went off. The big horse smelled the water and was anxious to get to the stream, but Jason held him back a moment longer to admire a scene, as pleasant as any he had seen in a long time.

As he sat engrossed in the beauty of the valley, a rider suddenly entered from the opposite end. Whipping his horse unmercifully, he raced for the trees along the stream, where the antelopes, suddenly frightened by the rider, scattered. Then a dozen or more riders came into view. Seeing the lone rider, they raced toward him with guns blazing.

Against such odds, Jason doubted the rider stood a chance, but whatever was at stake was none of his business.

In this country, a man fought his own battles, and a stranger interfered at his own peril.

The lone rider was almost to the stream when four riders broke from the trees and met him head-on. Now the man stood no chance, and even if Jason had tried to interfere, he would have been too late.

The man in peril pulled his mount up, jumped from the saddle, and grabbed for his six-gun. Kneeling in the deep grass, he returned the fire of the men closing in. A man with nerve, but one who stood no chance, Jason thought.

Some of the riders put extra shots into the prone figure before they rode off. Those shots weren't to make sure the man was dead. They were shots of malice, or so it seemed to Jason.

The party turned and headed in the direction from which they had come. When they were out of sight, Jason touched his knees to the sorrel and sent the animal down the slope, letting him set his own pace. A few minutes later, Jason was looking down at the dead man.

He was covered with blood from the dozen or so bullets he had taken, but his face was still intact. About fifty, his clothes were too expensive for a cowboy. A rancher, Jason decided. The man's horse, a blood-red bay, stood a few yards away.

Jason sat the sorrel a few moments, wondering if he should ride on or bring the bay in, put the man across the saddle, and take him to the marshal at New Castle, the nearest town. He settled on the latter and went for the bay.

He was about to lift the man across the saddle when a voice behind him said, "Reach, stranger!"

Jason froze and, his hands well over his head, slowly turned and stared into the muzzles of ten six-guns.

"Get down and take his gun, Big Zeke," a man, obviously the leader, ordered.

The man who gave the order was big. He was dressed in dusty range clothes and must have weighed well over two hundred pounds. He reached up and pushed a Texas hat to the back of his head, exposing black hair, a wrinkled brow, and intense black eyes in a fleshy face. Jason didn't care for the way those eyes were sizing him up.

Big Zeke was a lumbering, slow-moving giant with ham-like hands. His straw hat had a ragged brim that sat atop his big head as if it were a stranger to his red hair. His face was broad and reddish, with a slack look beneath a week's growth of red whiskers. His nose, obviously broken in the past, lay on the left side of his face. Lifting Jason's gun from its holster, the foolish-looking giant backed away.

"Look, I didn't shoot this man!" Jason said, finally overcoming his shock and surprise.

"Hand me his gun, Big Zeke," the leader said.

"Yes, sir, Mr. Blount," Big Zeke replied, and passed the gun up.

Ben Blount took the gun, aimed at the sky, and cocked the trigger six times. "This damn gun is empty," he said. He put the barrel to his nose. "And it's been fired recently." He turned to the man beside him. "Sky, you get down and help Big Zeke tie this jasper up. Bones, you and Hatfield get down and put Mr. Taylor across his saddle. Take the money belt from around his waist before you do. We'll take him and this jasper who shot him in to the marshal."

"You can't get away with a stunt like this!" Jason protested. "I saw you and your bunch ambush and kill Taylor, if that's his name!"

"You killed 'im and was in the act of robbing him when we rode up on you," the man called Blount said, an evil smile parting his thick lips. "Here's his money belt we took out of your hand. There's ten of us who'll swear to it in a court of law."

* * *

And swear they did, all ten of them. All, as it turned out, men rode for Evan Taylor's ET ranch, one of the biggest spreads in Southern Arizona and owned by the man Jason had seen them kill.

By the time Jason got the chance to tell his story, the only one who believed him was Rusty Hayes, the friend who had raised him. Rusty had got wind of Jason's troubles and come to see what he could do to help.

Rusty had lived on the farm next to Jason's father's farm back in Tennessee. He and Jason's father had gone off to the war together. When they returned, they were like brothers and never far apart. When the Wards decided to head West, it was understood that Rusty would come too. They had crossed Texas and were well into New Mexico when Kiowa Indians hit the small wagon train and Jason's parents and everyone one else in the train were killed. Without doubt, Rusty and Jason would have suffered the same fate had they not been out hunting fresh meat.

Jason had been happy to see Rusty walk into the courtroom. Ever since that fateful day when his parents died, whenever he felt hopeless, which was most of the time, he would turn and look into Rusty's wrinkled, trusting face.

There was more gray in Rusty's hair now and the lines in his face had deepened since Jason had seen him last. Though the word love had never been spoken between the two men, both knew it was there. Jason recalled the day he told Rusty he had decided to drift.

"I guess every man has a touch of the wanderlust," Rusty had said. "Your pa and me got rid of ours during the war. Thank God you can rid yourself of yours in a different way. You go ahead, son. Get it out of your system. When you get ready to settle down, you'll find a good place." Now the bond between them was even stronger, if that was possible.

The jury was out less than ten minutes and returned with a guilty verdict. Jason and everyone in the courtroom expected he would hang. But there must have been some doubt in Judge Thomas Blackburn's mind. Rapping his gavel on the desk for silence, he spoke the sentence.

"Jason Ward," he began, "I sentence you to ten to twenty-five years in Yuma prison. Take the prisoner away, Marshal Gruber."

Naturally, there were protests over what seemed a light sentence, but Judge Blackburn gaveled the noise away. Who knows what would have broken loose if the judge had let the crowd know that Jason could be paroled in five years if he caused no trouble. Of course, Jason didn't know that then, either.

Four days later, Jason was in a cell in Yuma Prison. He kept to himself, never speaking of his wrongful conviction or Ben Blount, but he vowed to take his revenge when he was free. He served his time in silence and, breaking no rules, waited for the day when he would be eligible for parole and could put into action the plan for revenge he'd planned all those nights lying awake in his cell.

One factor was critical: Blount must be perceived to be in the wrong, otherwise Jason would wind up in Yuma Prison again.

Chapter Two

Leaving the warden's office, Jason made his way to the front gate. He wasn't surprised when he saw the two men waiting there to say good-bye. They were the only friends he'd made during his five years in Yuma Prison. He had been hesitant in the beginning to let anyone get close to him but, eventually, had let his guard down, becoming friends with only two.

Mel Tenant had been his cell mate for the first two years. Mel was as slim and wiry as a vine. He possessed a narrow but handsome face with eyes that lit up when he laughed. He'd been in prison for six years when Jason had been assigned to the same cell. Mel had killed a deputy sheriff and had been convicted of manslaughter. He was up for parole in a few months himself when Jason's parole came through.

Jason already considered himself an old hand in prison when he met the other man, Stacy McCauley. Stacy was barely nineteen when Jason came across him in the yard.

All had made their living working with cattle. Having this in common, they became a threesome in the prison

10

yard—added protection against the sudden violence that could erupt at any moment.

"We gave the guard a week of smokes to let us come out and say good-bye," Mel said. "Hope you appreciate it."

"I do," Jason replied, shaking Mel's hand.

Turning to Stacy, he shook his hand and said, "You two take care of each other and look me up when you get out."

"You never said where you'd be," Stacy replied.

"I don't know yet," Jason answered, "but I'll let you know when I settle down someplace. So long for now."

"So long," both Mel and Stacy responded.

Stopping just outside the gates, Jason looked up. He had arrived at the prison after dark, and he had often sat in his cell calling up visions of what lay beyond the prison walls. He had missed a lot of things, and chief among them was a broad, sweeping blue sky such as he stared into now.

He wore the same clothes he had come to the prison in five years before. The only difference was the loose way they now fit his spare frame. He pulled the broad-brimmed, flat-topped hat low, partially hiding his prison-pale face. Women had sometimes admired Jason's features, but his face had grown gaunt from hard work and sparse prison food. Anyone who'd known him before prison might have seen the blond hair, deep forehead, and blue-gray eyes as those of a stranger. There was something even less familiar about the pale cheeks that sloped down to a stubborn-looking chin.

"You gonna just stand there and stare at the clouds all day?" said a voice Jason hadn't heard in five years.

Turning, he looked into the wrinkled face of Rusty Hayes. Rusty sat high in the saddle on a dun horse and held the reins of Jason's sorrel, who would now be nine years old.

Jason reached up and Rusty took his hand, holding it for

a moment. Rusty hadn't seen his friend in all the years Jason had been in prison because Jason had refused to let him visit, not wanting his old friend to see him in prison clothes or through prison bars.

"How did you know I was getting out today?" Jason demanded gruffly of Rusty.

"You wouldn't let me visit, but you never said I couldn't keep in touch with the warden," Rusty retorted.

"I might have known," Jason said.

"I wrote him from time to time to inquire about you," Rusty continued. "He was kind enough to let me know how you were doing. Seems Judge Blackburn took an interest too. I gather from the warden he had a lot to do with your parole."

"I have to check in with the judge when we get to New Castle," Jason said. "He'll be my parole officer."

The sorrel gave a familiar whinny, and Jason walked to the horse and draped an arm over his neck. The sorrel shook his head, turned, and gave Jason a nudge. He still remembers me," Jason said, and held the sorrel's head close, making a couple of soothing sounds.

"He didn't like it much, but I rode him from time to time to keep his wind up," Rusty said. "He's too fat and sassy. What that hoss wants are several long hard runs."

"Thanks for everything, Rusty," Jason said, looking at his old friend. "For keeping the horse safe and fit and looking out for everything while I was gone."

Climbing astride the sorrel, Jason sat a moment, enjoying the familiar feel of being in the saddle. Then he gave the Yuma Prison gates one final look, touched his knees to the sorrel's sides, and set out, Rusty following close behind. They headed east into a mostly empty desert.

They were well out of sight of the prison when Rusty

pulled up alongside Jason. "Maybe you better take this," he said, extending a holstered gun to Jason.

Jason took the belt and gun and buckled the belt around his waist. The gun was a Colt .45 Peacemaker. When he had bought the pistol, it was considered the best revolver manufactured. The weapon, whose knockdown power was tremendous, was well balanced and a quick second shot was easy. The black rubber grip with the design of an eagle on it had always been a comfortable fit for Jason's hand. He would need the gun when he set out on the course he had set for himself.

The gun and holster had been regularly oiled and obviously well cared for. He tried a couple of draws and was surprised at how natural the gun came into his hand. He would need some practice, but his skill at the draw would return soon enough.

"What do you aim to do about Blount?" Rusty asked. "That ET outfit's bigger than ever. They own just about everybody in New Castle now."

"I haven't decided yet, Rusty," Jason said. "I intend to put all that behind me if I can," he lied. "We'll just settle in and raise cattle. If he don't bother us, we won't bother him." Whatever came to pass, Jason didn't want to lose Rusty.

"Guess I'm a little surprised to hear you say that," Rusty replied. "But if that's what you want . . ."

"What about the ranch in New Mexico?" Jason asked.

"I sold it."

"How much did you get?"

"Ten thousand."

"Where's the money?"

"In the New Castle Bank."

"Well, the first thing we're going to do is buy us another ranch. I'd like to buy one somewhere around New Castle."

"New Castle suits me just fine," Rusty replied.

Chapter Three

Mountainous country lay west of Yuma, a country unknown to Jason, but Rusty had plotted out their course on a map. The first day out, they rode north of the Gila Mountains, passed those by, and, shortly before dark, camped at a water hole north of the Copper Mountains, a spot beneath an aging cottonwood with spreading limbs.

"You take care of the horses," Rusty suggested. "I'll get a fire started and cook up some supper."

"Suits me fine," Jason replied.

He stripped the horses of their gear, rubbed them down with handfuls of grass, and staked them out to graze. As he watched the horses, faint fingers of salmon pink reached up the sky from the lowering sun. The colors gradually changed to gold and then a deep red as the sun sank behind the Gilas.

The smell of boiling coffee and frying bacon reminded Jason they'd had only jerky washed down with water during the long ride. By the time he got back to the fire, his stomach was growling like two mountain lions about to fight.

"You getting hungry?" Rusty asked, eyeing Jason with a smile. "Sounds like two cats fixin' to fight in your belly."

"I smelled your coffee," Jason said.

Rusty pointed to the Dutch oven beside the fire. "Some fresh biscuits in there, and I'll make some gravy with the leavings after the bacon's done."

Jason ate a half-dozen biscuits smothered in gravy and a quarter side of bacon. When he was finished, he sat with his back to the cottonwood and sipped a third cup of coffee.

"Thanks for that meal, Rusty," he said. "Best I've had in five years. I may have to let my belt out a notch or two. Want me to clean up?"

"Naw, I'll do it," Rusty said. "You go out there, strip down, and set in one of them little pools where the water drains off. Take yourself a good bath. Wash that prison smell off you. A bath oughta make you sleep well tonight."

"You got any soap?" Jason asked.

Rusty tossed him a small jar of soft homemade soap. He took the jar and followed the stream until he came to a pool several inches deep and large enough to sit in. Stripping down, he knelt in the water, finding it cold enough to make him shiver. As soon as his body adjusted, he wet himself down and lathered up. Sitting on the sandy bottom, he washed the dregs of Yuma Prison from his hair and body, and for the first time he felt really free.

In the distance he could hear Rusty humming "Nellie Bly" as the old man worked about the camp. Rusty Hayes had been Jason's only family after the two had buried his parents. They had worked on ranches here and there, though often owners had refused to hire an aging cowpuncher with a kid for baggage. Spanish owners had been more sympathetic, and soon Rusty applied for work only on Spanish ranches.

When Jason was old enough to punch cattle himself, the

two had drifted back to Texas, stopping in the Big Bend area long enough to snare a small herd of wild longhorns from the brush around the fringes of the Davis Mountains.

Heading north with the small herd, they'd joined a cattle drive headed for Kansas. There they had sold the herd, ridden southwest to Cimarron in New Mexico Territory, and bought two thousand acres of empty land. They had started small, buying worn-out milk cows from settlers passing through and adding a bull now and then. They were running a thousand head when Jason decided he wanted to drift.

Jason returned from his bath wearing only long johns and boots. Rusty had already spread their bedrolls a few feet apart, and Jason shed his boots and lay down, using his saddle for a pillow.

"Enjoy that water?" Rusty asked.

"Best bath I've had in five years," Jason said, remembering how scarce water had been in the prison, though a river flowed nearby. Several men were forced to use the same tub of water, and Jason had known prisoners to fight over who got into the tub first.

"What was it like for you there, Jason?" Rusty asked. "What did you do to pass the years?"

Jason took a moment to think. "It was hell, Rusty. The worst part was the boredom. For the first two years, I stayed in a five-feet-by-eight cell twenty-three hours a day. Finally, I was let out into the yard more often. When I was in the yard, I spent a lot of time keeping out of trouble. Then I made a couple of friends and, together, we kept the bad boys at a distance. Strange as it seems, with the exception of you, I can't remember a single friend who isn't in Yuma Prison.

"As for what I did. There was a library with a few books. I read them all several times. When a new book came in, I got my hands on it as soon as I could. You ever hear of an English poet named Milton, Rusty?"

"Can't say I have."

"He wrote a piece called *Paradise Lost*. I'm not sure I understood everything in his poem, but I identified with the title. While I was in that cell, I missed all this. The springs, the trees, that mockingbird singing, the sounds of a horse pulling at grass. All that and more was the paradise I lost."

When Jason finished talking, he heard a familiar sound. Rusty was snoring. Well, so much for prison and John Milton. Jason rolled over and soon dropped off to sleep himself.

When Jason woke the next morning, Rusty had breakfast ready. He had reheated the coffee from the night before, and now it was so strong Jason almost had to chew it. There were flapjacks too. Rusty had even produced a bottle of syrup. Jason couldn't remember when he'd had a better breakfast.

Soon they were deep into desert country. In the early morning, the character of the desert was a different matter, presenting a rare kind of beauty. Before long, however, the sun began to sap the moisture from the flowers, low-growing shrubs, and stunted trees. Only the cactus remained strong and bold, having stored up reservoirs of water during morning dews and infrequent rains.

They were soon in country with which Rusty was familiar, and the old man pointed out the various mountain ranges and named them for Jason. Among these were the Mohawks, the Sierra Pintos, and the Granite Mountains, the latter no more than enormous piles of bare, black rock.

Then the land became a desert of brown lifeless grass, withered weeds, sickly saltbush, cactus, and scarlet-topped ocotillo plants.

"We made good time," Rusty observed as, five days later, they rode into New Castle.

A lot had changed since Jason had last ridden the streets of New Castle. Even some of the businesses he recalled had changed their names, taking advantage of the famous O.K. Corral fight between the cowboys and the Earps in nearby Tombstone. There was the O.K. Saloon, the O.K. Mercantile, and so on. When he mentioned this to Rusty, the old man muttered, "It's them writers. They come here by the drove to write about the doings of the Earps. Most of the books are tripe, but folks back in the East can't get enough of them stories. They've even started coming out here to see for themselves. You better steer clear of them, or they'll be writing about you next."

"Be a dull story," Jason observed dryly.

"Guess we better find us a place to stay," Rusty said, and pulled up before the O.K. Hotel. Leaving the horses tied to the rail, they went inside.

"Yes, sir! What can I do for you?" the clerk asked.

The clerk wore a black, threadbare suit with a high collar and a black string bow tie, and glasses. Weak gray-blue eyes squinted at them from behind the spectacles.

"Need a room for two," Rusty said.

"Sign here," the clerk replied, indicating a notebook.

"Room twenty-two," he said after they had signed. He took a key from a slot behind him and passed it over to Rusty. As they went upstairs, Jason glanced back and saw the clerk studying their signatures.

"Reckon he'll remember my name?" he asked Rusty.

"You kidding? He'll remember, and that fella is like a gossipy old woman. In an hour every jasper in New Castle will know you're back in town. But I reckon they gotta know sometime."

Once in the room, Jason washed his face and hands and beat the dust out of his clothes. Wiping off his boots, he turned to Rusty. "You got any money on you?"

Rusty produced several gold coins and gave them to Jason. "You going out?" he asked.

"Need to check in with Judge Blackburn. The money is for a new suit of clothes. I'll pay you back when I can."

"That's partly your money you'll be spending," Rusty replied. "Want me to go with you?"

"No, I got to learn to face the town on my own sometime. Might as well start now."

Jason wasn't sure what kind of welcome he would receive in New Castle. Still, his money was in the New Castle Bank—he'd had no choice but to return. Maybe he still had a few friends, even possibly Judge Blackburn.

Rusty was right. The clerk had already spread the word. As Jason crossed the street to the courthouse, he drew the eyes of everyone. Ignoring them, he entered the courthouse, climbed the stairs to Judge Blackburn's office, and knocked.

"Come in!"

Jason opened the door and stepped inside. "Afternoon, Judge."

Blackburn was a tall, distinguished-looking man. His well-trimmed thick hair was a lot grayer than when last Jason had seen him, and there were wrinkles about his eyes and across his forehead that were new as well. The blue eyes still retained their intensity, however.

The judge didn't seem to recognize Jason for a moment.

Then he broke into a smile and came around his desk. "Jason Ward! I've been expecting you. Had a letter from Warden Jones. He said you'd be looking me up."

They shook.

"Sit there," Judge Blackburn said, indicating the chair before his desk. Then he circled the desk and sat down himself.

"Well, you're out at last," the judge said.

"Thanks to you, Judge."

"Oh, I had nothing to do with the way you conducted yourself in there. You're the one who won the warden's trust."

Of all the people he knew, Jason knew he had to fool Judge Blackburn most about his future intentions. The judge was a no-nonsense law-and-order man. "Judge," Jason began, "I've served my time, and I have no reason to deny killing Evan Taylor. Still, I want you of all people to know I didn't kill him. You may still not believe me, but I told the truth on the stand that day. That's exactly what happened. Ben Blount and his riders killed Evan Taylor."

Judge Blackburn was silent for a moment. "I half believed you then, and I do believe you now," he finally said. "But there were all those witnesses who said they saw you do it. The town would have mobbed us both if I'd thrown the case out of court, and there was no way I could know for sure you didn't kill Taylor."

"Well, it's over now," Jason said. "Rusty and I have a little money from the sale of a ranch in New Mexico. I intend to get me a ranch, buy me some cattle, and settle down." Despite his vows of revenge, Jason half believed what he said himself.

"I like your attitude, Jason. Get on with your life and forget about the past."

Jason rose from the chair, and the Judge came from around the desk again and walked him through the door and into the hall. "I'll see you in a month," Judge Blackburn said.

Chapter Four

After five years in prison, even an ordinary thing like walking into a store felt strange to Jason. Choosing his own clothes felt even stranger. Strolling through the store, he came to the men's clothing section and eyed the selections. He chose two pairs of denim pants, two light blue work shirts, a blue neckerchief, and a brown canvas jacket for cool nights. After five years in a prison locker, his leather belt was cracked, and he chose one as much like the old one as possible. The black, wide-brimmed hat he'd owned for ten years still felt comfortable on his head, so he decided to make do with it for the time being.

A fresh-faced young clerk approached him. Jason, looking him over, wondered if he had ever looked so young. "Can I help you, sir?" the clerk asked.

"I'll take these," Jason said, laying his selections on the counter.

The clerk figured up the bill, and Jason counted out the money. "Can I change in here?" he asked.

"Certainly. Just follow me. I'll show you the changing

room." The clerk led Jason to the back of the store and indicated a curtained doorway.

Jason changed and, thinking he could still smell Yuma Prison on the old clothes, left them behind.

He felt like a different man when he emerged into the street again. Across from the mercantile shop was the OK Saloon. Jason waited for a couple of cowboys to ride past and then crossed the dusty street. Pushing through the batwing doors, he stopped and looked the room over.

The place had been remodeled since Jason last stopped in for a drink. Down front sat a half-circle bar that reached from side to side, leaving only enough space for doors at either end. Made from a dark wood, the bar was polished until it shone. A gold-colored metal foot rail circled the bottom, and the top was edged with the same metal. The bar stools, tables, and chairs matched the bar.

A half-dozen men stood along the bar and a poker game was in progress at one table. As Jason entered and walked to the bar, the usual noise ceased, replaced by whispers and then total silence. He stopped at the end of the bar, propped a foot on the rail and waited for the barkeep, who was serving another customer, to take his order. When the barkeep was finished, he approached Jason.

"What'll you have, Mr. Ward," he said, as though Jason had just been in the day before.

"A beer, Bolton," Jason said.

"Coming right up." The bartender turned, went back to the center of the bar, pulled a plug from a barrel, and filled a glass.

Bolton was tall, thin shouldered, and narrow waisted, with an unruly shock of hair. In the five years since Jason had seen him, the hair had gone mostly gray. He brought the beer, set it before Jason, then lingered. Jason lifted the glass to his lips and took a long, slow sip, enjoying the smoky taste of hops as it went down.

"Nice and cold," he said to Bolton.

"We keep the barrels in the icehouse out back," the barkeep replied. Bolton leaned in. "You maybe should get out of here," he said, swiping the bar with his rag and hardly moving his lips.

"That ain't friendly, Bolton," Jason said.

"It's a friendly warning," Bolton replied. "See that table of gents in the rear? They been looking you over since you came in. They're always picking fights. I think they got fighting with you on their minds now."

"Who are they?"

"They're ET riders," Bolton said.

Jason felt his stomach turn over. "Thanks for tipping me off, Bolton, but I don't have any beef with any ET riders."

"Don't mention it," Bolton said and gave Jason a curious look.

The ET men were reflected in the mirror, and Jason took a good look. They sat around a table on which stood several empty and half-empty bottles of booze. They were a salty, uncurried looking bunch, their hats mostly pushed to the back of their heads, their faces bearded and dirty. Some of the faces looked familiar, and anger stirred within Jason.

He had seen them from a distance five years back on the day Evan Taylor had been ruthlessly murdered. He remembered them from another time as well, on the witness stand, when, one by one, they had identified Jason as the killer.

Slowly, their names came to him . . . big, lumbering Zeke Colton, Sky Smith, and Richard Skeleton, a man whose flesh was so spare folks had nicknamed him Bones. The other two he didn't know or didn't recall. Jason felt the blood creep into his face as anger and hate boiled up inside him, becoming so strong he could hardly breathe.

Calm yourself down, he muttered beneath his breath. It was the most difficult advice to follow he'd ever given himself, but he reached for his beer, turned the glass up, and drank. Then, still looking in the mirror, he saw the five men push back, rise, and head for the bar.

Well, I won't be pushed too far, Jason told himself, and watched them come.

The man called Sky Smith led the pack, and they had Jason pretty well hemmed in when they stopped.

"Didn't know you'd have the nerve to come back to New Castle after what you done," Smith said, as though he didn't know he was a party to the murder he had helped to convict Jason of.

Smith was a long lanky galoot with a mean glint in his eyes which, at the moment, held an expectant look. Jason was sure the man was looking forward to starting trouble.

"Best advice I can give you," Smith continued, "is hightail it outta here before Ben runs afoul of you. He hates ex-cons worsen rats or snakes."

"You tell Ben Blount I don't mean any trouble for him or anyone else," Jason managed, controlling his anger with effort. "I'm looking to buy a ranch, settle down, and raise cattle and horses."

The saloon became so quiet, the drop of a pin might have been heard throughout the room. Men who knew Jason watched the confrontation with interest, sure that death, on one side or the other—maybe both—was only a breath away.

"He don't sound at all like he did that day in court when he told all them lies about us," Bones Skeleton said, a sneaky look beginning in his eyes and settling on his face.

"I'm not looking for trouble," Jason said, loud enough to be heard throughout the saloon. He wanted to make sure everyone got the impression he had tried to placate the ET men if he was forced to take action.

"He ain't looking to give us any trouble," Sky Smith chided, then added, "Maybe we should give *him* a little so he'll know what he's in for if he don't ride out of New Castle. What do you think, Big Zeke?"

That bear of a man had said nothing thus far and stood at the back of the pack. "Huh? What did you say, Sky?" he asked.

"This is the man who lied about us, Big Zeke," Bones said. "You gonna let him get away with telling lies on us?"

"He lied about us?"

"Sure as his momma's a slop eating dog," Bones replied.

Big Zeke pushed his way through to face Jason. "You said we lied?"

"Look, Zeke . . ."

"You shouldn't say that about us. Now I got to whup you."

Before Jason knew what was happening, the big man reached his hands out, caught the front of Jason's new shirt, and lifted him off of the floor. He suddenly found himself looking into the pale, almost expressionless eyes of the giant. Jason had been around hogs that smelled better.

The big man began to shake Jason, snapping his head back and forth. Jason wasn't sure he'd survive with his brains intact unless he did something. Meanwhile, the ET riders, as well as a few of the other men in the saloon, were cheering Zeke on.

Reaching for his beer mug, Jason smashed it against the bar, brought what remained up, and ground it across Big Zeke's face, leaving slivers of glass in his forehead. Then he raked it down, dragging the jagged glass across the big man's eyes and nose. Blood rushed from the cuts, filling

Big Zeke's eyes and running down into his mouth. Only then did the big man let go, dropping Jason to his feet again.

Before Jason could draw the Peacemaker, the others were on him. A fist smashed into his chin, sending streaks of light through his brain, and he fell backward. The steel-plated point of a boot found his chest, causing pain so intense Jason couldn't breathe for a moment. Someone lifted a chair and, had Jason not managed to move, the chair would have smashed down on his head rather than crashing against the bar.

The thought drifted through Jason's mind that if he didn't do something he'd die here on the saloon's dirty floor. *You gotta do something,* he told himself and, gathering all his strength, he pushed himself up, flinging his arms up and around, and brushed his tormenters aside for the moment. Then, curling his hands into fists, he struck out at a face directly before him. He heard bone snap as his fist landed against the man's jaw, and a howl of pain rose above the din in the saloon.

That yell gave Jason the moment he needed. Reaching for the Peacemaker, he hauled the gun out and rammed the barrel deep into the belly of Big Zeke. "Anybody move, I'll kill 'im!" he shouted, as sudden silence prevailed.

"Get him and your crowd outta here, Smith!" Jason shouted. "If anybody lifts a hand against me, I'll fill Big Zeke's belly full of lead!"

"And I'll be shooting too!" yelled Bolton, the barkeep. "Kill Ward if you want to, but do it some other place. I don't intend to be on my hands and knees scrubbing blood off my floor!"

Sky Smith made a halfhearted effort to pull Big Zeke back, but the big man brushed him aside and came at Jason again.

"Stay back!" Jason yelled.

But if Big Zeke heard, he gave no sign, and Jason squeezed a shot off point-blank at Zeke's shoulder. Big Zeke reacted to the shot as most folks would a bee sting and kept coming. Jason put a bullet into his foot, hoping that would stop him. It didn't. In fact, Big Zeke seemed suddenly to remember his own gun and, dropping a hand, drew it. Bringing it up, he squeezed off a shot that breathed past Jason's neck, the flash bright, the sound deafening.

Jason had had enough. He sent a bullet into the left of Big Zeke's chest that stopped him momentarily, but the big man still managed a couple of steps as his gun exploded again. The bullet hit the floor at Jason's feet, and then Big Zeke fell facedown on the filthy sawdust floor, making the building tremble.

Jason turned his gun on Smith and the others, expecting their hands to hold guns, but they had their eyes on Big Zeke, who let out a groan and lay still.

"That's enough!" someone shouted, and Jason turned to face a man with a star on his chest.

"You're under arrest," the man with the star said. "Give me your gun."

The star read "Marshal," and the man looked as if he could back up any pronouncement he wished to make. He stood about six feet and probably weighed 180 pounds. A Texas sombrero sat atop a head of thick black hair, and a thick handlebar mustache curled up from his thin lips as dark, smoldering eyes bored into Jason's.

He wouldn't mind shooting a man, Jason thought. "Sure, Marshal," he said, handing him the Peacemaker, butt first. "I don't think we've ever met. My name is Jason Ward."

"Boyd Gruber, and we've met," the marshal replied. "I was marshal here when you went off to prison." Taking

Jason's arm, Gruber pushed him through the crowd and out onto the street.

Jason recalled Gruber then. In fact, Gruber had arrested him five years earlier, and within days he was off to Yuma Prison. Would that be his destination again? So soon?

Chapter Five

"Morning, Ward," Marshal Gruber said as he approached the cell door carrying a tray covered with a red checkered cloth.

"Morning, marshal," Jason replied courteously.

Gruber slid the tray beneath the cell door and stepped back. "Reckon you'll be on your way to Yuma Prison soon," he said. "Killing a man is a sure way to break your parole."

"They had their mind set on killing me, Marshal. Big Zeke would have finished me in short order if I hadn't shot him. All you have to do is ask folks who were in the saloon."

"None of that may matter," Gruber said. "You killed an ET man. If the law were to turn you loose, the ET crew would come after you. Anyways, the ET folks swear you had it in for Big Zeke because he was in the bunch that saw you kill Mr. Taylor. They say if they hadn't jumped you in the saloon, you'd have killed them all."

"But others were there, Marshal. Will you ask them?"

"I could ask, but whether or not the killing was justified

isn't the point," Gruber replied. "You're charged also with disturbing the peace. That's enough to send you back to Yuma. Now eat your breakfast before it gets cold." Turning, Gruber walked back toward his office and out of sight.

Jason was awakened the next morning by the marshal opening the cell door. "What now, Marshal?" he asked.

"The charges against you have been dropped," Gruber said. "You're free to go."

"You could've done that last night," Jason said, "if you'd asked around a little."

"I got a word of advice for you, Jason."

"What's that, Marshal?"

"If Yuma prison didn't leave you senseless, you'll get out of New Castle as fast as a horse will take you. You got about as much chance of staying alive here as a snowflake in hell."

"Then the law should protect me," Jason said, smiling.

"I intend to try, but I don't stand a chance against the ET crew. They'll catch you alone or ambush you. Since Blount took over, that's a mean and dirty bunch. If I had my way, I'd run them out of the county."

"Thanks for the advice, Marshal," Jason said, and followed Gruber to his office to receive his personal possessions.

Jason found Rusty and Judge Blackburn waiting for him. They rose to greet him. "Might have known you two were behind my getting out, and I thank you both."

"Give Rusty the credit," replied the judge. "He's had a string of people coming in here all morning telling the marshal who was at fault last night. I merely came along to make sure the marshal understood what they were telling him."

"You doing all right, Jason?" Rusty asked.

"I had to kill that fella, Rusty, or he would have killed me. I'm still a little shaky from that, I guess."

"You did what you had to do," Rusty replied. "Everyone knows that, and there's a lot of talk around town now about what Ben Blount will do to you if he gets the chance."

"Then I'll have to be careful," Jason said. "But thanks again, and thanks to you, Judge."

Judge Blackburn left them outside and returned to the courthouse. As Rusty and Jason watched him go, Rusty said, "We better talk to someone about ranches for sale around here, unless you've decided that coming back here is a mistake after all."

"Who would that be?" Jason asked, ignoring the latter part of Rusty's statement.

"Reckon Jim Tolbert at the bank would know about such things," replied Rusty. "We'll drop in there."

They walked the block to the bank and entered. The one window was open but no one appeared to be behind the cage at the moment.

"Can I be of service, Mr. Hayes?" asked a studious-looking man behind a desk to their right.

"Came to see Tolbert," Rusty said.

"I'll tell him you're here."

He rose and entered a door behind him. The printing on the door read *Jim Tolbert, Bank President*. A moment later, the man returned. "He'll see you now," he said and left the door open.

Jim Tolbert had come to town after Jason went to prison. He proved to be an impressive-looking man. He wore a three-piece gray striped suit, a white shirt, and a black string bow tie. Unparted, graying brown hair was slicked back on his head. The forehead was smooth, eyebrows thin, nose prominent, chin rounded. A smile exposed very white teeth. His eyes were brown with a secretive gleam.

"What can I do for you, Mr. Hayes?" he asked, pumping Rusty's hand.

"Want you to meet my partner, Mr. Tolbert," Rusty said. "This is Jason Ward. Jason, this is Jim Tolbert."

The only sign Tolbert gave that he had heard the name before was a sudden sharpening of the eyes. Jason waited for the banker to extend his hand. He did after a moment's hesitation, his grasp a little too firm, as if to impress Jason with his manly strength.

"I'm pleased to meet you, Mr. Tolbert," Jason said.

"Same here, Mr. Ward."

Tolbert moved back behind his desk. "Have a seat," he said, indicating two chairs, as he plumped himself down in his own high-backed leather chair.

"Now," Tolbert said, "what can I do for you gentlemen?"

"We're looking for some ranch land to buy," Rusty said.

"What size ranch did you have in mind?"

"Guess that'll depend some on the price," Rusty replied.

"Did you have some location in mind?"

"You got a map of the county?" Rusty asked.

Tolbert took a map from a desk drawer and spread it over the desk.

"You show him where we have in mind, Jason," Rusty said.

They both rose and walked to the desk where Tolbert had spread the map. Jason hadn't seen a map of the county in a long time, but the lines marking the rivers and roads were familiar. He spotted the valley he still remembered after five years and moved his finger to the spot.

"This valley here, if it's for sale," Tolbert said. "Some told me you once made some improvements on it, but your claim has lapsed. Most of that country belongs to the ET spread, as I'm sure you know, but no one has since filed on the valley you claimed. It's for sale, and there's a couple of thousand acres of good grass and plenty of water. Would you be interested in buying it?"

"I would," Jason said.

"We could ride out and take a look in the morning," Tolbert offered.

"That would be fine," replied Jason.

"About eight o'clock then. Meet me at the livery."

"We'll be there at eight," Rusty told him.

Rusty and Jason had their mounts saddled and waiting when Jim Tolbert came. He rode a spirited black gelding that had Kentucky racing horse written all over him. Tolbert himself wore eastern riding clothes. His black hat had a wide Western-type brim to keep the sun off his neck and face, however.

"Nice day for our business," he said.

"Couldn't be better," Rusty replied.

"And you, Mr. Ward? How do you find the world outside of prison walls?"

"That's all behind me," Jason replied, a bit surprised by the question. "I want a chance to live peacefully, hopefully on my own ranch, with Rusty here."

"And good luck to you in that endeavor," the banker said. "Now let's be on our way."

The ride took them into the desert and toward some distant low hills. In the early morning the desert lacked the heat a clear sky would bring later in the day, and Jason enjoyed the coolness while it lasted.

Soon they came upon withered cholla cactuses, big clumps of prickly pear, and huge yucca plants. Jason took note of the lizards and scorpions one found in the desert. Though they were ugly creatures, all tough skin, horns, and ridges, he couldn't help but admire them. They lived and prospered in an environment in which few other animals could exist. A little like Yuma Prison, he thought to himself.

As they neared the line of hills, brown grass became slightly more plentiful, and the desert plants seemed to lose their hold on the terrain. When they finally topped a ridge overlooking the valley, the country below changed dramatically.

The scene, after five years in prison, was even more beautiful. Tall cliffs and hills surrounded several square miles of grass, belly deep to a horse. As Jason had pictured in his mind so often, a stream cut through the valley, and along its banks grew tall cottonwood and, lower down, the soft green of weeping willows. Below Jason was the spot where Ben Blount and his riders had caught up to Evan Taylor and riddled him with bullets.

"How much?" asked Rusty.

"Seven thousand, and not a penny less."

"That's too much!" Rusty exclaimed.

"Six thousand, and not a penny more," Jason offered.

Tolbert looked at Jason and then Rusty.

"You heard him," said Rusty.

"You've bought yourself a ranch," Tolbert said.

Jason was pleased with the purchase, for he had always known the valley would be a fine place to raise cattle, but more importantly, he was aware of how close the ET spread and Ben Blount lay. It should be easy to provoke Blount into some kind of action. But Jason wasn't unaware of the danger to himself. Blount had the great odds of money and men at his disposal. When he took the bait and came after him, Jason might be the one not to survive.

Then, anger surged up inside Jason. This county was his home. He had a right to buy a ranch and live here. If the ET tried to drive him out, he'd meet them head-on. A fight might mean Yuma Prison again, but he had survived that hellhole once already. He could again.

Chapter Six

The heat was intense, but Jenny Taylor thought she'd take the heat anytime over the dust kicked up by the wheels of the stagecoach and the pounding hooves of the team. The dust penetrated everything: her blouse, her stockings, her shoes, and even her mouth. With distaste she swiped her moist face with a handkerchief and then fanned it back and forth a few times.

Her thoughts returned to the orderly, pleasant home of her aunt in Philadelphia, and she suddenly longed to be back there again. She had dreaded the afternoon teas and the many dull concerts, but just now they seemed quite an attractive alternative to the jolting coach on little more than a trail.

Despite her present disheveled condition, Jenny Taylor had grown into a beautiful young woman. Her linen suit revealed a slim waist and inviting curves. At five-nine, she was a little tall for a woman. She sat with her hat in her lap, and thick blond hair hung in curls to her shoulders. Her blue eyes were framed by long brown lashes, but her eyes were not her only striking feature. A master painter couldn't have arranged the pert nose, firm lips, and slightly squared chin into a more beautiful combination. A complexion a shade darker than the blond hair and without a blemish held the features together.

The coach had left Phoenix the night before. According to Tee Martin, the driver, they would reach New Castle sometime before dark. Tee really stood for Tory, a name the old man had hated all his life, and he had threatened more than once to shoot anyone who called him by it to his face. Few remembered his real name anymore, however, and the occasions for Tee Martin making good such threats were few and far between, since he was known by all as Tee.

Tee was pushing fifty. He had driven stagecoaches for thirty years, first out of Fort Worth, then Abilene, his wanderlust moving him west as the railroad crossed the continent. Finally, tired of moving around, he had settled in Phoenix.

He was a wiry man, not quite six feet tall, weighing just shy of a hundred and fifty pounds. His thin hair was the color of weathered wheat and contrasted oddly with his darker brows and the thin mustache decorating his upper lip. His face was sunburned and wrinkled, reminding Jenny of drying mud cracked by a hot sun. He had the voice of a much larger, thicker man, a clarion voice, developed over the years from shouting at stubborn, contrary mules and horses.

His usual garb was a dusty, sweat-ringed Texas hat, a faded blue neckerchief, a faded red shirt, and faded denim pants tucked into half boots. Some folks thought he had only the one suit of clothes, but the truth was he had several, all exactly the same and with about the same degree of wear.

A Winchester leaned against the seat beside his leg, and

he wore a bullet belt and holster, the latter holding a Colt .45 six-gun. He had been forced to use the guns from time to time over the years, both of which he used very well, as many bandits and holdup artists could testify.

Jenny had liked the old man from the beginning. Though his talk was sometimes a little rough, he came through as a kindly man and, to Jenny, he epitomized the Western men she remembered from her youth—rugged men, sometimes lacking polish, but men to whom women were something precious to be protected from all harm. Priding herself on her independence, she wasn't too much enamored of the latter idea, since she felt she was able to take care of herself. But she knew there was little she could do to change the concept.

When he took over in Phoenix, Tee had seen each passenger into the coach, introducing himself to each. When Jenny had told him her name, his face had brightened. "From New Castle?" he asked.

"I used to live there, but I haven't been home in many years."

Tee's thin lips stretched into a smile. "Would you be the daughter of Evan Taylor?" he asked. "The daughter who went off east to school maybe ten years back?"

"Yes, sir, I'm Jenny Taylor."

"Then I knew your father," the old stage driver said, his expression turning sad.

"Do you know how he died?" Jenny asked. "The letter from his banker back then just said he was dead. That's been troubling me for years. When my Aunt Effie died a few weeks ago, I decided to come home and find out and see what happened to the ranch."

"You mean you don't know?" Tee asked, surprised.

"The letter I had from a Mr. Jim Tolbert, a banker, just

said he was dead. He mentioned nothing about the ranch, and I was too young to think much about it. As I grew older, I began to wonder more and more. I might have come home earlier, but toward the end my aunt was sickly. She had raised me from the age of ten, and I felt obliged to look after her. Was there something wrong about my father's death?" she asked.

"Your father was murdered, Miss Taylor," Tee said, his voice reflecting his sadness at delivering such sad and shocking news.

"And the ranch?" she asked, not seeming surprised at the news about her father.

"According to what I heard, your pa left it to his foreman, a man by the name of Ben Blount."

"Who murdered my father?" she asked.

"A man by the name of Jason Ward was sent to prison for it, though he denied doing it. In fact, he accused Ben Blount and his riders of the murder. Said he saw them do it."

That conversation had kept Jenny's mind busy as the dusty miles passed, and Tee had become more and more solicitous of her welfare with the passing of each mile. First, he felt guilty at being the one to tell her of her father's murder. Then, the more he got to know her, the more he liked her. If he'd had a daughter, he had told himself more than once already, he would want her to be exactly like Jenny Taylor. And the closer they came to New Castle, the more concerned he became for her and her safety.

As uncomfortable, dusty, thirsty, and tired as she was, and despite what Tee had told her, Jenny still felt a growing anticipation as the stagecoach neared New Castle. When she had been sent east to live with her Aunt Effie, her-father had promised she could come home for Christmas from time to time, but something kept interfering when a trip was planned. That day ten years ago when, with tears in her eyes, she had waved good-bye to her father had remained with her all these years, and she could still recall the love in his eyes when he had kissed her good-bye.

For a year or so she had been homesick for her father and the ranch but, as she came to enjoy school more and more and the company of her Aunt Effie as well, the ranch, her father, and Arizona Territory had become less and less important, finally fading into a warm memory. When her aunt died and Jenny was free of the responsibility of caring for her, her mind had turned once again to her father and the ranch. The following day she had left Philadelphia by train. A week later she was within a few miles of New Castle and, hopefully, the answers to the questions that bothered her.

Aunt Effie, a thrifty woman, had refused to spend any of the twenty-five thousand dollars the banker had sent in a second letter, saying it came from the sale of the ranch. Her aunt had seen that the money was invested wisely, and Jenny was now considered a wealthy young woman.

Throughout the long ride from Phoenix, Jenny had helped to occupy the time by conversing with her two fellow passengers. The more pleasant of the two was a middle-aged woman with the definite look of a spinster and strong opinions on most things.

"I'm a schoolteacher," she told Jenny. "My name is Irma Mason. I'm to take over the school in New Castle. I do hope it's a nice town."

"I'm afraid I can't tell you much about New Castle," Jenny replied. "I haven't lived there since I was ten."

"How about you, sir?" Irma Mason asked the other passenger, a man who sat across from her.

The man, a tall thin fellow, replied with a grunt that might have meant anything, and soon the two women gave up trying to involve him in their talk. Nor did Jenny like the covert glances he gave her from time to time.

"Tell us about New Castle," Irma asked Tee during a stop to allow them to stretch their legs.

"Ain't much of town," Tee replied. "Some good people and some bad, like every town I suppose. Got a lot of nice kids though. I expect you'll enjoy teaching most of them."

"I'm sure I will," Irma said, deciding she'd find out what New Castle was like soon enough anyway.

The sun was maybe an hour high when the stage pulled into New Castle. Tee pulled the team to a stop, climbed down, and came to the stage door to help his lady passengers down.

"You got a place to stay?" he asked Jenny when he took her arm and helped her through the stage door.

"I supposed I might find a hotel nearby," she replied.

"You wait right here," he told her. "I'll turn this team over to someone and see you get a room. Won't do for a pretty young thing like you to walk along the streets by herself so near dark."

"But I don't want to put you out," Jenny protested. "And what about Miss Mason?"

"Members of the board of education will see to her," Tee replied. "See? Some of them are talking to her now."

Jenny turned back for a look at Irma and found that, indeed, what Tee said was true. Two men, one with Irma's bag, were escorting her to a carriage. She also saw the unpleasant man who had been a passenger talking to four men who stood at the hitch rack where five horses were tethered. While she watched, the tall man turned and gestured toward her. The other four followed the tall man's gesture with their eyes. Jenny found herself feeling uncomfortable under their stares. Who were these men? A sudden sense of danger stirred within her. She brushed the thought aside. What could happen to her in the middle of the town?

"And you won't be putting me out," Tee continued. "Why, I'll be the envy of every man in New Castle who sees me walking along-side you."

"You are a very gallant man, Mr. Martin," Jenny said, and smiled.

"I'd like you to do me a favor if you will," Tee said.

"You've only to ask."

"I'd be obliged if you didn't call me . . . uh. . . . Just call me Tee, like everybody else does."

Jenny laughed. "I'll call you Tee if you call me Jenny."

"You got yourself a deal, young lady," Tee replied with obvious pride.

Tee, carrying her bags, led Jenny along the dusty main street of New Castle and stopped before the O.K. Hotel. "About the best rooms in town," he said, opening the door and following Jenny inside.

"A room for the lady, Sampson," Tee called to the clerk.

Jenny watched the man's expression change as he turned and looked at her. She noted the threadbare condition of his suit and weak gray-blue eyes that suddenly came alive behind the thick lenses of his spectacles. She couldn't help wondering about the effect a woman, even a stranger, had on men in New Castle.

"Yes, ma'am," the clerk said and hastily arranged the book for her to sign.

Tee, still carrying her luggage, led the way upstairs to her room which overlooked the street along which they'd just come. Opening the door, he stepped back and allowed

Jenny to enter. He followed and placed the luggage at the foot of the bed.

"Would you ask the clerk to send a tub of hot water up so I can take a bath?" she asked.

"All right, and I'll come for you in a couple of hours," replied Tee, "and we'll get something to eat."

"Why, I'd like that very much, Tee," said Jenny. "I'll get myself cleaned up and be ready. And Tee, thanks for everything."

"Ain't done nothing," Tee said, his dark face turning red as a beet. He backed out of the door, closing it after him.

The tub of water arrived soon, carried by an elderly black man whose ebony face was framed by hair as white as cotton. "You need anything else, miss, just let old Moses know."

"Thank you, Moses."

The tub proved too small for Jenny to sit down in, but she managed to stand and wash the dust from her body, feeling fresher than anytime since she'd left the hotel in Phoenix. She decided to dress conservatively for dinner and, opening her luggage, chose a dark green blouse and a tan skirt. Next she slipped on half-length brown riding boots and, brushing her blond hair until it shone, she tied it off with a green ribbon.

She was still trying to grasp the implications of what Tee had said about her father's death. Who was this Jason Ward who'd been convicted of his murder? And why had not Jim Tolbert, the banker, told her that in his letters long ago? Now she had heard for the first time that Ben Blount, her father's foreman, had inherited the ranch.

She had a vague memory of Blount, a big, rough man of whom she'd always been a little afraid. She didn't recall her father being so fond of him. She wondered, given what had happened to her father, if she'd been wise to return. If her father had been murdered, might she not be in danger herself?

The thought was a little frightening. Crossing to the window, Jenny stared down into the dusty town. At the end of the street, a few shimmering heat waves seemed to lend an apprehensive feel to the town, a sense of foreboding. A rider passed beneath her, the hooves of his horse kicking up spurts of dust. When she heard Tee knock, she crossed to the door, opened it, and invited him in, feeling relieved by his homely presence.

"Where are we eating?" she asked, slipping a shawl about her shoulders.

"The O.K. Café," Tee Martin told her.

Jenny laughed. "Why is everything in New Castle called O.K. something or other?" she asked.

"After that famous gunfight between the cowboys and the Earps over in Tombstone," Tee explained a little gruffly. "They fought it out at the O.K. Corral. The newspapers and them writers back east made quite a thing out of that shindig. Even here in New Castle, the merchants think they can use the name to snag a few strangers in for some business. Me, I think they're just being foolish."

"How nice you look, Tee," Jenny said, taking note of the new pin-stripe suit he was wearing.

Tee's reply was an embarrassed grunt and a loud clearing of his throat. He felt like a different person in his new clothes and a little foolish as well. But he couldn't take a young lady to supper without dressing up.

The cafe was about half full, and their entrance brought a sudden silence in which every eye turned to the door and settled on Tee, and then stayed on him, with quick glances at Jenny. Apparently, Tee's new clothes were creating more of a sensation than a strange young woman, something that pleased Jenny. She held Tee's arm even tighter as a waiter led them to a table, where Tee held a chair for her to sit.

"Why are they staring at you, Tee?" she whispered teasingly when they were seated.

"At me? Bunch a durn jackanapes if you ask me," muttered Tee. "Reckon they ain't used to seeing me in one these newfangled suits."

"You got dressed up for me, didn't you, Tee?" she asked, reaching out to touch his rough, weathered hand.

"Couldn't see a lady to dinner in rags, I reckon," he said, and Jenny was sure she saw a mischievous gleam deep within the old man's sunken eyes.

The lady who brought the menus took a look at Tee and stopped in her tracks. "Why Tee Martin!" she exclaimed. "I didn't recognize you all dressed up like that. Thought a stranger had wandered in. Somebody must've died, and you've just came from the funeral."

"Now, Bertha, ain't nobody died," Tee said, embarrassed. "You act like you ain't never seen a man in a suit before."

"Ain't never seen you in a suit before, Tee Martin," the lady said, placing the handwritten menus before them. "And how long have I known you? Must be most of thirty years now."

"Jenny, this is Bertha Dawson," Tee said, introducing the two women. "Bertha, this is Jenny Taylor. You'll recall the little thing Evan Taylor sent off to stay with her aunt and go to school. She came in on my stage today."

Bertha Dawson was a trim woman of maybe fifty years. Many considered her a little pushy, but Jenny liked the friendly smile on her face and had enjoyed her good-natured kidding of Tee. "Nice to meet you, Mrs. Dawson."

"Same here, and you're a pretty young thing, my dear. You'll drive the cowboys into fits when they get a look at you, and I can understand why this old goat here got all dressed up."

"Why, Bertha, I ain't no goat," Tee protested, "and why don't you just tell us what's good tonight like you usually do when I come in?"

Bertha flashed Jenny a smile. "The stew's good, Tee. I had some myself. There's some fresh sourdough bread and coffee made not ten minutes ago. That suit you?"

"I reckon," Tee muttered.

"Sounds good to me too," Jenny said.

Bertha gathered the menus. "I expect you're in town alone," she said to Jenny, "else you wouldn't be out with this old desert Romeo."

"I am, and Tee here has been very kind to me."

"What I wanted to say is I remember what happened to your father," Bertha continued. "If you need a woman friend while you're in town, you just come to me."

"Why, thank you, Mrs. Dawson," Jenny said, touched.

"Call me Bertha."

"And I'm Jenny."

"Well, Jenny, you just remember what I said."

"Looks like you made yourself a friend," Tee said, looking fondly at the retreating back of Bertha Dawson, "and you couldn't make a better one." he added.

"I can use some friends," Jenny replied.

Loud laughter erupted from a table across the room, and Jenny glanced in that direction. Two men, dressed in dusty range clothes, returned her glance and broke off their laughter. One was the man who'd been on the stage with her.

"Who are those men, Tee?" she asked.

Tee Martin turned and looked at the men. "Name of Sky Smith and Bill Hatfield."

"Who are they?"

"Some of Ben Blount's men from the ET spread."

"From what used to be my father's ranch?"

"Some of the same bunch Jason Ward claimed killed your pa," he answered. "Don't pay them no mind. It's the likes of them that makes the streets unsafe for respectable women."

Chapter Seven

The long, steamy stage ride had begun to catch up with Jenny, and Tee returned her to her hotel room after they had eaten. "I think I'll go right up," she told Tee when they entered the hotel and Jenny led the way upstairs.

"Sorry I won't be around tomorrow," Tee told her at her door. "But I got to take the stage back to Phoenix. But you just remember, girl, if you need any help, you can call on old Tee when I'm here."

"Thanks, Tee. Thanks for everything." Reaching up, she planted a quick kiss on his wrinkled cheek.

Five minutes later she was undressed and in bed, hoping for a good night's sleep. But though she was tired, she had too much to think about for sleep to come easily. The uneasy feeling she'd had when Tee had told her of her father's murder came to her again, and she wondered what would happen if she poked too deeply into her father's reason for leaving the ranch to Ben Blount.

What if the man who'd been convicted of killing her father was right? What if Ben Blount was the murderer? Could he have somehow gained ownership of the ranch by murdering her father? A sudden chill took possession of her, though the blanket was tucked snugly beneath her chin.

Maybe I should turn around and head back to Philadelphia, she told herself. *After all, I don't need the money.*

But she knew she wouldn't. Curiosity about the last few years of her father's life had brought her here, and she wouldn't leave until she had looked into what had happened to him.

Before she went to sleep, she laid out her course of action for the next day. First, she would visit the marshal. Then she'd go to the bank and talk to Jim Tolbert. Finally, unless she was satisfied, she would ride out to the ranch and speak with Ben Blount. Exhausted, she turned on her side and drifted off to sleep.

She had breakfast the next morning at the same cafe where she and Tee had eaten the night before. The place was empty except for Bertha. Jenny took a stool at the counter to save the woman some steps.

"Need some breakfast, I'm guessing," Bertha said.

"I know it's a little late, but I hope you're still serving," Jenny replied.

"I can rustle you up a slice of beefsteak and some eggs. How would that do."

"If you could add some coffee to that," Jenny said, "it would be perfect."

When Bertha set the plate of steak and eggs before Jenny, she filled two cups with coffee, placed one beside Jenny's plate and, bringing the second cup with her, came around and sat beside Jenny. "Are you planning to come back to New Castle and live?" she asked.

"I'm not sure yet," Jenny said. "I've been curious for a long time about how my father died and why he didn't leave the ranch to me."

"But he did leave you something, or so I heard," Bertha said.

"And quite enough too. I know my father loved me, and yet he never let me visit after he sent me away. My aunt was a dear woman, but when she died, my mind turned more and more to my life here with my father.

"Then yesterday Tee told me he'd been murdered. Now I'm more curious than ever. Why wasn't I told about that? And did my father's murder have anything to do with Ben Blount getting the ranch?"

"But Ben Blount had nothing to do with your father's murder," Bertha said. "Another man was convicted of that and sent off to prison."

"So Tee told me, a Jason Ward."

"He's out of prison now, you know."

"He is?"

"Yes, I see him in town from time to time."

"Maybe I'll talk to Mr. Ward as well," Jenny said thoughtfully. According to Tee, the man had denied killing her father. But didn't all murderers deny their crime?

"Where is the marshal's office?" Jenny asked when she had finished breakfast and paid her bill.

"Go outside and turn to your left," Bertha told her. "You'll see his shingle a block down."

"What's his name?"

"Boyd Gruber."

"What kind of man is he, Bertha?"

"Honest and conscientious, as far as I know. There are some who don't like him, but I suspect they've run afoul of the law at one time or another."

Jenny found the marshal's office as directed. She had never had contact with anyone connected with the law before, and she was a little nervous as she entered.

The man behind the desk made her even more nervous. His big hat was pushed to the back of his head and held there with a string tied beneath his chin. His black hair was neatly combed, and at the moment his eyes were on a paper on the desk.

"Marshal Gruber?" Jenny asked timidly.

Stern dark eyes looked up at her and then turned friendly. Then the lips beneath a thick mustache curled into a smile. Jenny managed to relax a little.

"What can I do for you, miss?" the marshal asked, rising.

"I'm Jenny Taylor. I'd like to ask you some questions about my father, Evan Taylor."

Marshal Gruber rose at once and removed his hat. He was surprised, to say the least. He had only recently released the man who had killed Evan Taylor from his jail. Now he was confronted by Taylor's daughter wishing to ask questions which would, no doubt, concern his death.

"Won't you have a seat, Miss Taylor?" he asked, indicating one of the chairs before his desk.

"Thank you, Marshal."

"Now, about those questions?" Gruber asked, sitting again himself.

"Just how did my father die, Marshal?"

"He was ambushed and shot near his ranch. The man who shot him was convicted and sent off to prison."

"I understand he's out now. How could that be?"

"He was convicted of second-degree murder, got from ten to twenty-five years, and was paroled recently for good behavior."

"Doesn't seem fair, does it, Marshal? Someone murders a man and goes free after only five years."

"There are some . . . prominent men who think Ward didn't murder your father," Gruber said.

"Then who do they think did?"

"Ward himself has always claimed that Ben Blount and the ET riders did the murder. But Blount and his men all swore at the trial that they saw Ward waylay your father and shoot him."

"Then as far as the law is concerned, it's all settled and over?" Jenny asked.

"A man was tried and convicted. As far as the law is concerned that settles it."

Jenny was silent for a moment. "Do you know why my father left the ranch to his foreman, Marshal?" she asked.

"I looked into that at the time, Miss Taylor. Your father's will was very specific. He wrote of the great debt he owed his foreman."

"What was the debt?"

"The will didn't say. As far as I know, no one ever heard your father speak of it. Maybe Blount just did a good job for Mr. Taylor. Maybe your father thought you weren't interested in coming back here to run a ranch."

Jenny rose. "Well, thanks for your time, Marshal."

"Will you be staying in New Castle?" Gruber asked, following her to the door.

"I haven't made up my mind yet. Good day to you, sir."

"Good day, miss."

There seems no need to talk to Mr. Tolbert, Jenny thought to herself. *But I think I'd like to hear what Ben Blount has to say. I'd liked to know more about the debt my father owed him.*

Chapter Eight

Rusty and Jason spent their first few days cutting poles for a corral so the horses wouldn't have to be hobbled at night. When the corral was finished, they started cutting and hauling logs for a barn. Using sod for a roof, the barn took only a few days to build. With shelter for their saddles and warbags and a permanent home for the horses, they began to think about a house.

"Let's throw up something temporary so we'll have some shelter," Rusty suggested. "Then we can take our time and build something really nice and permanent."

Jason had worked at building around the prison, but then he had built without taking much care. These buildings were to be home for him and Rusty though. In fact, as he became more and more engrossed in the work, he thought less and less about Ben Blount.

"Time we had some cattle on this range," Rusty announced one day.

"Reckon so," Jason replied.

"We got everything a cow could want right here," Rusty continued. "Plenty of grass, fresh water, and shade. Cows shouldn't want to wander. Anyways, them hills all around make a natural fence."

"Where might we find cattle to buy?" Jason asked.

"We got a few things to do before we start looking," Rusty replied. "I'd like you to ride into town and look up a blacksmith. Have him make us a branding iron. You can register the brand while you're there."

"What's our brand to be?"

"How about the WH connected?"

"For Ward and Hayes. But maybe it should be the HW connected—Hayes and Ward."

"I got it right the first time, boy," Rusty said gently. "You're going to be here long after I'm gone. Your name should come first."

"You'll outlive me, you old codger," Jason said.

Jason went to New Castle the next morning. As he rode down the main street, he was aware that folks still scrutinized him. He doubted that people would ever get over the fact that he was an ex-con—more specifically, an ex-con who had supposedly murdered a man who was a leading member of the community.

He saw the blacksmith shop and pulled up. The sign above the building read *Blankenship Blacksmith*.

Stepping down from the sorrel, he walked beneath the open shelter and found a man tapping small strips of iron into nails. He had the biggest, most muscular and hairy arms Jason had ever seen He was stripped to the waist, and sweat dripped steadily from his face, arms, and chest. The smell of hot iron and burning coals permeated the barn.

"Come in, stranger," the man said, "and tell me what I can do for you."

"Need a branding iron," Jason told him.

The blacksmith ceased his work and looked at Jason. "Name's Blankenship," he said.

"Jason Ward."

Walking to a water bucket that hung from a hook, Blankenship reached for a dipper and took a healthy drink. "Care for some?" he asked, offering Jason the dipper.

"No, thank you."

"Now what you want on that iron?" Blankenship asked, going to a bench and returning with pen and paper.

"WH Connected," Jason replied.

"The W would be for Ward," Blankenship observed, "but who would H be?"

"Rusty Hayes."

"I know Rusty. Somebody was telling me he had bought himself a ranch, and they mentioned a partner. You tell Rusty to come see me if there's anything I can do to help you gents get started."

"I'll give him the word, Mr. Blankenship, and thanks. Of course, we'll be needing to buy some starter cows soon," Jason said.

"How many?"

"That'll depend on the price, but a good starting number would be in the vicinity of a hundred. We'll be needing some bulls too."

"You know Lester Beatty?" Blankenship asked.

"No, sir."

"Rusty knows him. Lester was in here yesterday. He's looking to sell off some of his herd. Lester Beatty has some of the finest shorthorn cattle around. You tell Rusty to look him up."

"I'll tell 'im, and thanks. When can I pick up the branding iron?"

"You can kill a couple of hours and drop back by."

Jason considered stopping into one of the saloons for a drink. Then he thought of what had happened the last time and rejected that idea. Instead, he decided to drop by Len Conklin's mercantile and pick up some supplies.

After Jason bought coffee, bacon, flour, and several cans of peaches, he saw a row of books and, selecting several, asked Conklin to include those in his purchases.

"You a reading man, Ward?" Conklin asked.

"Kills time in the evening," Jason said, "and I had a lot of time for reading when I was in prison."

Conklin seemed surprised at the easy way Jason spoke of his past. "Seems to me," he said, "you'd have picked some other place to settle after you got out. Some of the people around here don't look kindly on your coming back here."

"Look, Mr. Conklin," Jason said, looking the merchant in the eye. "I never killed Evan Taylor, but I was convicted of his murder anyway. I was sent away, and I've served the time they gave me. You tell folks I didn't come back here to start trouble. I'm partners in a ranch. All I want to do is work it in peace." He hoped Conklin believed him.

"Reckon you better tell Ben Blount that," Conklin said. "He's doing a lot of talking against you when he's in town."

"I don't reckon I could tell Blount anything," Jason said.

"Were I you, I'd keep an eye on him," Conklin replied.

Jason was surprised to get such a warning from Conklin. On top of that, there seemed to be an absence of malice in Conklin's words. "You got something I can carry all this in?" he asked.

Conklin supplied him with a couple of flour sacks and helped to fill them with the books and the groceries. Then Jason tied the top of the bags together with a piggin string so he could drape the bags behind his saddle.

Sky Smith and a couple of other men were dawdling

before the doors of the O.K. Saloon when Jason rode past. They became silent when they saw him. Sky Smith hitched his gunbelt up a couple of times, the move suggesting he was tempted to take Jason on then and there.

"Won't be Big Zeke you'll be facing next time," he called to Jason's back.

Jason made no reply and kept the sorrel to a steady walk, watching Smith from the corner of his eye.

When Jason reached the end of the street and made his turn, he glanced back. Smith and the two riders had mounted. They sat their horses in the middle of the street, staring after Jason. They were still there when Jason passed from sight.

He was halfway home when suddenly he got the feeling he was being followed. The feeling persisted, and he remembered the attention he had received from Smith and the others earlier that day. He decided to travel with more care, keeping watch among the trees and surrounding hills on either side. At the same time, he was busy with his thoughts, but never forgetting to remain alert. Still, he saw no movements and heard no sounds that were alien to the scene. Several times he saw antelope and deer, and once a coyote fled into the brush at his approach, creeping deeper as he waited for Jason to pass.

His eyes were searching the terrain ahead when he saw the wrecked buggy maybe a quarter mile down the trail. The rig was turned on its side, and the position of the horse suggested the shafts were broken and possibly one of the upright wheels as well. A woman stood with her hands on her hips and stared at the wreckage. Obviously, she hadn't the slightest idea what to do.

Touching the sorrel with his heels, Jason sent the big horse toward the wreck. Pulling up, he took in the wrecked carriage and the scuffed condition of the lady's clothes. "Ma'am, can I be of help?" he asked.

"I hope so," she replied. "A rattler spooked the horse, and I couldn't keep him on the road. My name is Jenny Taylor. I'm on my way to the Taylor ranch, and I would appreciate your help."

Her identity came as a shock to Jason. He remembered her as a small blond child around the ranch's premises when he himself was a teenager. Assuming what her reaction would be if she heard his name, he purposely didn't introduce himself.

He was impressed with her manner, however. Obviously, she was a lady of quality, and beautiful at that, and she appeared down to earth, neither flustered nor unnerved at the situation in which she found herself. Jason liked what he saw in her.

Swinging down from the sorrel, Jason slipped his knife from its sheaf and walked to where the buggy horse struggled. Since the animal didn't appear hurt, he knelt and slit through the harness with his knife, freeing the horse. When the horse struggled up, Jason reached for the reins and kept him from running.

"I'll see you home, but you'll have to ride a horse," he said, eyeing the outfit she was wearing.

"That won't bother me," she replied, "though I would prefer a saddle of some kind."

Jason saw she was contemplating riding the buggy horse. "My sorrel has a saddle. You can ride him. I'll ride this one."

"Would you?"

"You bet," he said and adjusted the sorrel's stirrups for her.

"Would you allow me to help you up?" he asked.

"That won't be necessary," she replied, and stepped

quickly to the sorrel, reached for the horn, and breasted herself into the saddle, exposing calf-length boots and neat inner knees.

Jason felt himself blush. Then he thought of what Jenny Taylor would think of him once she knew who he was, and he forced any thought of them being friends from his mind. Jenny had settled into the saddle so naturally, Jason had the impression she'd ridden astride many times before.

Jason climbed astride the buggy horse, hoping the animal would behave. And he did, plodding along beside the sorrel like the stolid old fellow he was.

They rode for awhile in silence, each apparently busy with their own thoughts, and Jason was impressed by the calm, simple way Jenny accepted his help, not as if it were due her, but in a way that suggested he might be a neighbor.

"Why didn't Blount or one of the men meet you in town?" Jason finally asked.

"No one knew I was coming."

He had heard vaguely that she was somewhere in the East, and he'd been under the impression she wasn't expected to return. He couldn't help but wonder why she had come back unannounced.

"Guess you intend to surprise them," he said.

She didn't reply, and Jason didn't press her with more questions.

The sun was almost overhead, but enough wind drifted through a nearby hogback to ruffle the grasses and hold the heat in check. Overhead, a hawk rode the same currents. He was low enough for Jason to see the constant swivel of his head as he checked the terrain for prey. Either the shadow of the hawk or the bright sunshine kept the small land animals at bay, however, and the hawk finally drifted off to more promising hunting ground.

Jason, probably because of his preoccupation with Jenny, had forgotten the feeling he'd had earlier that someone was dogging his trail until he heard an explosion from the crest of a nearby hill and saw dust kick up near the feet of the sorrel. Ramming his heels into the sides of the buggy horse, Jason reached for the sorrel's reins, intending to take both horses into the thick willows and cottonwoods along the stream. Before he could grab the reins, however, Jenny gave the horse a command and streaked for cover. Jason followed on the lumbering buggy horse as more bullets kicked up dust behind and to either side of the old horse.

When they were safely behind cover, Jason stepped to the sorrel and jerked the Winchester from its sheath. He found a clearing he could shoot through and sent a couple of bullets at the hilltop where the ambushers had waited. He thought of Sky Smith and the men who had followed him out of town. Or had they been following him? Could they have been following Jenny Taylor?

"I think it's safe for us to go," he told her.

The Taylor ranch house was no longer the same place Jason remembered. In the five years since he had ridden past, the house and grounds had gone to seed. The yard was overgrown with weeds, and broken-down equipment was strung out between house and barn.

Evan Taylor had had finished lumber hauled in from a sawmill down near the Rio Grande when he built the house, and back then Jason had never seen it without a fresh coat of paint. Now the paint hung in peeling shreds. Windows which had once sparkled from constant cleaning now had panes missing.

The barn and corrals were in even worse condition. Saddles were thrown haphazardly about, and bridles were carelessly slung across corral poles. Many of the posts sagged to one side, and some of the lower poles of the corral were broken. He'd never seen a place in such a rundown condition, and anger rose within him that anyone would allow a ranch to deteriorate to such a state.

Apparently, they were expected, for Ben Blount was waiting in front of the house.

"What're you doing here?" Blount demanded of Jason. "Who gave you permission to ride onto this ranch?"

"I did," Jenny said. "I had some trouble coming out from town and wrecked the buggy I rented. This gentleman was kind enough to help me." Jenny swung expertly from the saddle and faced Blount.

Jason swung down too. "Meet Miss Jenny Taylor, the owner," he said to Blount.

The change in Blount was too quick. Such a sudden transformation suggested to Jason just how devious the man could be. Now Blount couldn't have been more respectful. Moving in closer to Jenny and removing his dusty hat, he said, "You should have let us know, ma'am. We'd have met you in town."

"This place looks a mess, Mr. Blount," Jenny said. "It was never like this when my father was alive. Why aren't you keeping the place up?"

She was putting up a good front, Jason thought, but Jason could tell she was nervous.

"I got some problems," Blount said, "but nothing I can't take care of. I'm just short on cash at the moment."

"Reckon I'd better go," Jason said. Readjusting the sorrel's stirrups, he climbed aboard. Then, looking down at Jenny, he asked, "Would you like to ride back into town with me?"

"I came out to talk to Mr. Blount," Jenny said. "I'm sure

he'll lend me a saddle horse to ride back to town when I'm ready. But thanks for your help." Turning to Ben Blount, she said, "Where can we talk, Mr. Blount?"

"Hold on a minute," Jason said. "I'm not sure I should leave you out here."

Jenny knew what he meant. After all, Blount was the man she believed had killed her father. But if she was to learn anything from Blount, she had to talk to him alone.

"Who appointed you my keeper?" she asked icily. "Nothing's going to happen to me here. Am I right, Mr. Blount?"

Ben Blount seemed to do a couple of mental shuffles. "She'll be safe with me and my men," he said.

"All right," Jason said, doubtfully. He turned the sorrel around and rode toward town.

When Jason looked back, he saw Jenny Taylor picking her way through the litter in the yard to the house, her skirts lifted to the top of her boots. Blount was following her.

As Jason rode toward the WH Connected, he wondered again if the attempted ambushers had been Sky Smith and the men with him. If so, he had just left Jenny Taylor in a den of wolves. But what else could he have done, short of forcing her to return to New Castle? Surely not even Ben Blount would harm a woman who the town folks knew had gone to consult him. If he did, the men of New Castle would stretch his neck from the nearest tree limb.

Chapter Nine

As Jenny moved up the cluttered walkway to the front door, she was amazed at the memories the walkway and the house revived. She recalled playing with her dolls in the sandy yard. After rains she would make sand cakes and bake them in the sun. And she remembered the many times she had met her father as he came in from the meadows. He would lift her in his arms, swing her back and forth, and then carry her inside, her squeals of delight echoing throughout the house. The memories were suddenly so vivid, tears came to her eyes.

Blount opened the door for her, and she stepped inside. She thought the front room seemed the same, but that couldn't be said for the condition of the furniture. The same stuffed chairs, the tall fireplace, even the pictures of long dead ancestors on the walls were there, all covered with a deep coat of dust. Cobwebs hung from ceiling to floor.

She turned to face Blount and said with as much composure as she could muster, "Suppose we talk here, Mr. Blount."

"And what did you want to talk to me about?" Blount asked, his voice filled with nervous bluster.

"What was the debt to you mentioned in my father's will, Mr. Blount?" Fudging a little with the truth, she continued, "He wrote to me often, and he never mentioned any debt. I have come here to learn what that debt was."

The light in the room was dim, but Jenny saw the sudden change that came over Blount. Instead of the subservience he had shown upon her arrival, he became more the man she remembered. For a moment, the fear he had stirred in her as a child returned. But was there something suggesting fear in Blount's eyes as well?

"What kind of things did your pa say in those letters?" Blount demanded.

He *was* afraid, Jenny decided. His fear came from her mention of her father's letters. Could he be afraid that something in those letters contradicted her father's will? If that were the case, had the will that gave him the ranch expressed her father's real intent? Suddenly, she was afraid and wished she'd had been content with Marshal Gruber's explanations and never come to the ranch.

Her fear caused her to move toward the door, and she knew she wouldn't ask Blount for a horse to ride to town. She'd ride the buggy horse, even without a saddle. As she attempted to pass by Blount, he reached a hand out and caught her.

"Where are those letters?" he asked, squeezing her arm.

Anger overrode her fear for the moment. "Let me go, sir!" she demanded.

"Tell me about those letters," Blount ordered, shaking her roughly. "What did your pa tell you about the ranch in them letters?"

"He never mentioned the ranch in his letters," Jenny said,

reversing herself. "Now, please, turn me loose. I'm expected back in town before dark."

"You ain't going nowhere till I know what's in them letters! Did you show them to anyone yet?" he asked, his rancid breath playing across her face as he continued to shake her.

"No! I don't even have them with me! I left them in Philadelphia!" Jenny managed to say.

"You're lying, woman!" he shouted. "Them letters are in town, ain't they? You brought them with you to prove that old man didn't leave me the ranch! Ain't that right? Tell me the truth, or I'll shake your teeth loose in your head!"

When she didn't answer, Blount flung her hard to the dusty floor and stood over her. As he glared down at her, Jenny saw in the man something wild and savage, and she knew she looked up at a man who would kill her if he didn't get what he wanted. She also knew as surely as she lay on the floor in the dust that the wrong man had been convicted of her father's murder, the wrong man sent to prison. But now she was afraid to tell Blount the truth . . . that she had no such letters from her father. He might not believe her anyway.

"Reckon I'll have to keep you here till I can send someone into town and get them letters. You're staying at the hotel, ain't you?"

The fall had left Jenny's ears ringing, and she felt sure she was about to faint. Then Blount lifted her to her feet and, shoving her along before him, moved her down a hallway which Jenny only barely remembered. At the end of the hall, he opened a door and pushed her inside.

"You ain't leaving here till I get my hands on them letters," he said. He closed the door, and Jenny heard a lock click.

Still dazed by Blount's brutal treatment, Jenny stood in the center of the room, shaken by the stunning turn of events. Crossing back to the door, she tried the knob and found the door locked, as she had known it would be. From the door she went to the window only to see a man suddenly appear outside. Lifting a rifle, he pointed the weapon at her, gave her a sinister smile, and shook his head. Jenny retreated and sat on the edge of the bed.

Somehow I have to get out of here and get back to town, she told herself. *After what's happened to me, maybe I can convince the marshal that Ben Blount was the man who killed my father.* But how was she going to escape though a locked door and a guard at the window?

Pacing back and forth, she tried to think. Then she realized she was in the room she had occupied as a child! From all appearances, the room had not been cleaned in many years and the same cobwebs and dust were everywhere. Yet there was no mistaking the room. She had slept in this room until her father sent her away.

She had loved the room and suddenly recalled the many happy hours she'd spent there, playing all sorts of imaginary games and poring over books. Another memory that surfaced was of her rock collection. She had spent hours searching the ravines and gullies near the house for smooth pebbles of different shapes and colors. She had pretended the rocks were nuggets of gold and had hidden them away. But where? Then she remembered. Going to the wall, she searched for a certain board which had two sections. Kneeling, she lifted the lower end of the board and reached inside.

The first object she brought out was the ragged doll she had slept with for years. Her father had forbidden her to carry the doll to Philadelphia with her, so she had hidden it in her secret place to keep the doll safe. Next, her hand found a piece of folded paper. Puzzled, she brought it out. The paper was an envelope addressed to her. Opening the envelope, she unfolded a letter and began to read.

Dear Jenny,

You may never see this. But if you ever return, maybe you'll remember your secret place. I don't think I ever told you I knew about it. The truth is I fear for my life. You may not remember Ben Blount, my foreman, but he has tried most every way under the sun to convince me I should leave the ranch to him. Till now I have refused, but I think he may resort to force. If something happens to me and you return and find this, take it to whoever is marshal in New Castle. Don't trust Jim Tolbert. I think he may be involved in the scheme.

Love,
Your father, Evan Taylor.

Jenny, still on her knees, was stunned. She thought of Blount. If he found the letter and knew she had read it, her fate was sealed.

Somehow she had to escape and get the letter to Marshal Gruber. If she couldn't get to town, maybe she could find the ranch belonging to Jason Ward. Ward certainly had the right to evidence that proved him innocent. Rising, Jenny refolded the letter, returned it to the envelope, and stuffed it in her blouse.

The question now was how to escape.

Chapter Ten

After locking Jenny in the room, Blount stepped outside the house and yelled for Sky Smith. When Smith came from the bunkhouse, Blount walked to meet him.

"You want something, boss?" Smith asked.

"Yeah, I don't want that girl going back to town. I've got her locked in a room at the end of the hall, the one with the light. I put one of the boys on guard, and I want you to keep one there. You tell each guard, if that girl gets past him, I'll have his hide."

"But, boss, people in town will miss her. They know she came here, and they'll come asking questions. What about that Ward fella? Some of our boys might not like it. You're apt to have a mess on your hands."

"I don't care what the boys like or dislike, and Jason Ward wouldn't come around if you and the boys had taken care of him. I don't like a man who fails, Sky. I don't like that at all."

"Sorry, boss, but Ward is as slick as a cat. He seemed to know we were on the ridge even before we began shooting. The woman took off like a bat out of hell, and Ward was right behind her. Wasn't nothing we could do after he got in the trees. We'd a' been killed ourselves if we had rushed him then."

"Nothing but excuses, Sky. I may get a little tired of that one of these days," Blount snapped.

The two men walked back to the bunkhouse together. Though Blount now owned the ranch, he still slept in the foreman's room at the front of the building and ate with the men as well. This preference of his was the reason the house was so run-down.

Smith had always thought Blount's not moving into the house was a little strange. It was as though Blount thought Evan Taylor might return to haunt the house. But making the girl a prisoner was stranger still. Something drastic had to be at stake for Blount to take such a risk.

Smith had had his own suspicions about the will that gave Blount ownership of the ranch. Smith had helped kill Evan Taylor and had been well paid for his part in the plan, as had the other riders which Blount had brought in. But that will had come as a surprise to all of them. Now Smith's suspicions were strengthened. The girl was a threat to Blount. Could she somehow prove the will leaving the ranch to Blount was false?

Maybe, maybe not, but Blount had to be desperate to keep that girl prisoner here. If the men in the community found out, Blount would be in for a world of trouble. There had to be some way he could profit from this himself, and Smith vowed to put his mind to exactly how.

"Don't forget," Blount said as they entered the bunk-house, "I want a guard under that window at all times."

"I'll see to it, boss," Smith replied as Blount pulled open the door to his small room, went inside, and closed the door after him.

"You," Smith said to a swarthy-looking puncher who was sprawled on his bunk. "Git on up to the house. The girl's locked in one of the rooms. You find out which one and relieve the guard that's posted under her window after a few hours. And stay outside, you hear? No messing around with her."

The puncher was one of the ones who had eyed Jenny Taylor so hungrily. Now Smith's warning put an idea into his head. "Right away, Sky," he said and, grabbing his hat and his rifle, went outside and headed for the house.

Later that night, Blount sat at a small desk in the foreman's room. Once in private, he let his uneasiness show, and his face reflected his fear of what would happen if he were caught holding Jenny Taylor prisoner. Pushing back from the desk, he paced up and down the small room a couple of times before he sat down again.

Then, picking up some papers, he tried to focus on the figures there. Records had proven the bane of his existence since he had taken over the ranch, but, he had managed to keep abreast of what it was taking in. Tonight, though, he couldn't concentrate.

He knew Smith was right. People in town would miss Jenny Taylor, and someone was bound to come searching for her. Still, if he turned her loose, she would ride back to town and tell everyone that Jason Ward had been right, that Blount had killed her father. There was no way he could allow that to happen.

But could she prove it? Wouldn't it boil down to his word against hers? And, again, there were the men. They had been involved in the killing too. For a few hundred dollars he could insure that any number of them would swear they had heard Evan Taylor talk of willing the ranch to him.

Still, he'd be taking a chance. With Jason Ward back

and telling everyone again and again that he was innocent of killing Evan Taylor and saying repeatedly that Blount was the guilty one, the girl's story might sound more convincing. No, he had to get rid of her, just as he had to get rid of Jason Ward.

He recalled when he first got the idea of taking over the ranch. Evan Taylor had been very much alone after he had sent the girl to school in the East. Except for the girl, Taylor had no family, and as Blount worked his way up on the ranch to become foreman he had managed to get rid of riders loyal to Taylor, replacing them with men loyal to him.

All the while, Blount had gradually lined his pockets by running off a few head of cattle from time to time, curbing his greed for the whole shebang until the right time came.

Blount had met Jim Tolbert in the O.K. Saloon one night. They'd had a few drinks and played some poker. Before the night was over, Blount had caught Tolbert dealing from the bottom. At first, he was furious that a banker would cheat. But Blount had kept his silence, sizing the banker up as someone he might be able to use in his scheme to take over the Taylor ranch.

Finally, after several more poker games in which Tolbert continued to cheat, Blount had spoken to him about the idea of forging a will. At first, Tolbert had seemed outraged at such an idea. When Blount confronted him about his cheating and threatened to spread the word, Tolbert caved in. In nothing flat, the banker had become enthusiastic about the plan, providing he received a sufficient reward. Tolbert had found someone to forge the will, or forged it himself. Blount had never known for sure.

Bringing his mind back to his present problem, Blount remembered the wreck Jenny Taylor had mentioned. What if she were found dead under that wreck? Who could say she hadn't been killed when the buggy overturned? Ward, of course, the man who had found her and brought her to the ranch. But if Ward were dead too. . . . He had to keep the girl alive until Ward was killed, but that could be done quickly enough.

Blount put his plan into action that very night. First, he called Sky Smith and Bones Skeleton to his room. "How would you boys like to own Ward's and Hayes's spread?" he asked. "I get word they're about ready to put cattle on it."

"How we gonna get hold of that ranch?" asked Bones, the greed apparent in his eyes.

"We'll get rid of Hayes and Ward," Blount said. "Then we'll have Jim Tolbert fix up a bill of sale. You can swear Ward and Hayes sold us the ranch and then left town with the money."

"How are we gonna kill them jaspers?" Smith asked. He had already failed at killing Ward once.

"We'll take every man we have, raid their place, kill them both, and burn the place down," Blount told them.

"But won't folks get suspicious when we turn up with a bill of sale?" asked Bones.

"Not if Jim Tolbert is a witness to the sale. In fact," Blount continued with a smile, "with that bill of sale we can point out we had no motive to kill them and burn the place down, since we'd already bought the place. We'll say Ward must have burned it to get back at me."

"Damn it, Ben," Smith said, "I think that will work, but won't we have to give the rest of the boys something?"

"I reckon so," replied Blount. "When the deed is done, I'll give each man three hundred dollars. You two will have the job of making sure they all accept."

"And if there's one who doesn't agree?" asked Bones.

"Then you know what to do with him. Shoot 'im and put him six feet under."

"When will we do the job?" asked Bones.

"When I say the word," replied Blount.

There was still the matter of the letters, but with Jenny Taylor dead no one would pay any attention to letters written years ago by a man who was also dead. If someone did, there were ways of handling them.

Chapter Eleven

Chase and Rusty called on Lester Beatty, bought the cattle that same day, and brought them home. The cattle took to the valley as if it had always been their home. First, smelling the water, they went to the stream to drink. Then, a few settled down in the shade of the cottonwoods, while the rest drifted out to graze. Rusty and Jason sat and watched for a while, enjoying the satisfaction of the moment.

Though the ranch Jason dreamed of would soon become a reality, there was still a lot of work to be done. But Jason couldn't get Jenny Taylor off his mind.

"You better ride into town and see her," Rusty said, his comment taking Jason by surprise.

"See who?" Jason asked, trying to sound innocent.

"You can't fool me, boy," Rusty said. "I've known you from the day you were born. You been worrying about that girl all day since you left her at the Taylor place. You won't be worth nothing here till you go into town and see if she's all right."

Jason needed no more urging. Putting everything aside, he saddled the sorrel.

"Maybe I should go with you," Rusty said, after following him to the barn. "Never know who you might run into in town."

"Might look like I had to have a chaperone when I call on a girl, Rusty. But I'll be careful not to pick a fight with any ET riders if I run into them."

"If you ain't back by night, I'll come anyway," Rusty said. He stood in the yard and watched Jason ride off, a concerned look on his face.

As Jason rode toward New Castle, clouds began to drift in from the northwest. At first, they were merely white and fluffy, but soon they became more numerous, finally merging into one huge storm cloud with an ominous black underbelly.

"A storm is coming up, old fella," he said to the sorrel. "Maybe we better push along a little faster."

The cloud continued to build and draw near even as the sorrel complied with Jason's command. Soon dark clouds had hidden the sun, and Jason was happy to ride into New Castle. When he pulled up before the O.K. Hotel, the rain began to come down hard. Swinging from the saddle, he stooped beneath the rail, stepped up on the boardwalk, and entered the hotel.

"Miss Taylor's room," he said to the clerk.

"Why, she ain't in her room," the clerk replied.

The clerk's words sent a surge of dread through Jason. "Where is she then?" he asked. "Has she left town?"

"If she did, she didn't take her clothes with her."

"What's been done to find her?" Jason asked.

"I told the marshal she hadn't come back," the clerk said. "He rode out to the old Taylor ranch looking for her. That's where she said she was going when she rented the buggy from Charlie Lambert. He found the wrecked buggy, but there was no sign of Miss Taylor, and Mr. Blount said he hadn't seen her. Folks are afraid she wandered off afoot and got lost, not being in this country since she was a little girl. Today the marshal and some men are out scouring the country for her again."

I saw her going into the house with Blount, Jason thought to himself. *Blount could have decided she meant some kind of threat to him and kept her there. Either she was still there or she was no longer alive. Despite her ugly words to me, I should have picked her up and put her on the horse and brought her back with me,* he thought to himself. But surely Blount would know better than to harm her. The men of New Castle would stretch his neck from the nearest tree limb. Maybe she had decided of her own accord to stay at the ranch. After all, it belonged to her.

With Marshal Gruber out riding the country looking for her, Jason had no alternative but to ride to the ET ranch himself. If Jenny wasn't there, he would force Blount to tell him where she was or what had happened to her.

Chapter Twelve

The rain had stopped by the time Jason reached the Taylor place, but with the sun just set, the buildings and grounds were shrouded in twilight. He pulled up before the house and glanced around. He could see some effort had been given to making the place look more presentable, and a dim light shone from inside the house. Swinging down, he wrapped the sorrel's reins around a hitch post, walked up the path to the door, and knocked.

When the door swung open, he was face to face with Ben Blount. Jason palmed the Peacemaker when he saw Blount's hand dip to his holster. Thrusting the gun into Blount's belly before Blount's gun cleared leather, Jason stared Blount down.

"What're you doing here again, Ward?" Blount demanded with his usual bluster.

"I came to see Miss Taylor," Jason said.

"She ain't here."

"Where is she? She hasn't made it back to town yet."

"How should I know? She came in and asked me a few

77

questions about Mr. Taylor's will. I answered them and she left. I already told Marshal Gruber that."

"Did he search the house?"

"There was no need for him to do that," Blount replied. "He knows I wouldn't harm a lady like Miss Taylor."

"You better not be lying to me," Jason told him, taking the Peacemaker from Blount's belly. "If you're telling me a lie, I'll be back."

"You can take a flying leap, you!"

Jason brought the Peacemaker down against the side of Blount's head with all the force he could muster. Blount gave a grunt as his knees folded. Jason left him lying there, half in and half out the door.

Jason had only ridden a couple of miles when bolts of lightning split the dark sky and thunder rumbled across the heavens. "Looks like we'll get some more rain," he said to the sorrel. He had hardly spoken before a burst of strong wind brought a chilling rain that beat against the already wet ground, quickly forming puddles. Even before he could untie his rain gear and get into it, Jason was soaked.

Ordinarily, he would have ridden to his ranch for dry clothes, but the rain offered the best chance he might have of searching the Taylor place for Jenny without being discovered by Blount and his men. They would all be inside out of the rain, and Jason would be free to move about. Turning the sorrel around, he retraced his steps.

Leaving the horse in a grove of scrubby oaks, Jason made his way down a slight slope to the house, coming in from the rear. When he reached the house, he pulled up close and tried to merge with the wall. Between the house and the barn was a long building Jason recognized as the bunkhouse. From the bunkhouse came the sound of a guitar and someone singing a cowboy song. Other than that, the only sound Jason heard was the rain.

Slowly, he began to inch his way along, keeping as close to the house as possible. The windows were mostly dark and, when he peered inside, he could see nothing. Nor could he hear anything when he pressed his ear to the glass.

Finally, he reached the corner of the house and peered around. Light fell through a window and onto a man pacing back and forth below. Jason watched him pace a couple of times, the sound of the rain pelting the man's slicker noisily. Waiting for him to make his turn at the spot nearest him, Jason stepped out quickly, gun in hand. When he was within reach, he brought the Peacemaker down on the back of the man's head.

Certain he had hit the man hard enough to keep him out for some time, Jason stepped to the window and looked in. Jenny sat in a chair beside the bed with a book in her hand. Gently, he tapped on the glass. When she turned and looked, he motioned for her to come to him. Together they lifted the window, and Jason helped her through.

"Thank God you've come!" she whispered.

"We'll talk later," Jason said, hurrying her along. "Right now we've got to get out of here before that guard comes to or his relief shows up."

When they reached the sorrel, Jason lifted her into the saddle, then he climbed up behind her. Circling her body with his arms, he took the sorrel's reins and turned the horse toward town, the warm, compact body in his arms sending shivers of heat through his belly.

Jason, remembering she didn't know his name, was tempted to tell her who he was, but he held back and Jenny began to talk.

"Blount knows I think he killed my father," Jenny said

after a few minutes. "They convicted an innocent man and sent him off to prison. One of the first things I want to do is find Mr. Ward and tell him that. Where is his ranch?"

"We'll be riding there in a few minutes, Miss Taylor."

"To Ward's ranch? But why? I thought we were on our way to town."

"Right now what we both need are dry clothes. We can get those at Ward's place. I'll take you into town tomorrow."

Jenny suddenly became quite still in his arms.

"Is something wrong?" he asked.

"You're Jason Ward, aren't you?"

Jason was startled for a moment, wondering how she'd figured that out. But there was no longer any use in denying it. "Yes, ma'am," he said.

"Why didn't you tell me who you were?"

"I was afraid of how you might have reacted, knowing I was the man who had been convicted of killing your father."

"Wait till I show you what I found," she said.

"What?"

"A letter to me from my father. He hid it in a secret place in my old room, thinking I might find it if I ever came back to the ranch."

"What does the letter say?" Jason asked.

"That my father was afraid Ben Blount was planning to kill him and take over the ranch."

The skies were clear when Jenny awoke the next morning. She lay in a bedroll beneath a tent. Beyond the tent she heard birds singing, and someone was humming a tune that sounded familiar. She could also smell food cooking. She threw the bedroll aside and pushed herself up. Rusty, closer to her size than Jason, had loaned her a shirt to sleep in. Her own clothes, now dry, lay just inside the tent. She slipped out of the shirt, dressed, and left the tent, following the smell of food cooking to the shade of the nearby cottonwood.

Rusty gave her a plate of beans, bacon, and a slice of bread. Someone had placed some rocks beneath the tree, and Jenny sat down on one and began to eat. Rusty poured himself a cup of coffee from the large, smoke-blackened pot that sat on the bed of coals and came to sit on the rock nearest her.

"Where's Jason?" she asked.

"He's scouting around in case Blount may have got some idea you came here," Rusty said. "He said for me to tell you to be ready and, when he gets back, he'll take you into town."

For a moment, Jenny felt disappointed. She had sensed last night that Rusty Hayes possessed many of the traits she had liked so in Tee Martin, and she felt drawn to him. And Jason? What could she say about him? He had spent five years in prison for a crime he hadn't committed and, as far as she could tell, he harbored little bitterness toward anyone, with the exception of Ben Blount.

But she had seen something in Jason Ward's eyes each time Blount's name was mentioned, a quiet sort of rage, though outwardly he showed little hate or resentment. When she had shown Jason her father's letter, she had expected to see some of that rage let loose, but his only reaction had been a stiffening of the jaw. She felt sure, however, that sometime Jason Ward would make Blount pay for those years in prison.

"I knew your pa, you know," Rusty said, breaking into Jenny's reverie.

"When? Where?" Jenny asked.

"We rode with a posse after a bunch of renegade Comanches who did some raiding up along the Cimarron," Rusty said. "And I ran into him a few times after that. Evan Taylor was a fine man, but I guess you know that."

"I didn't know him at all during his last years," Jenny replied. "As you know, he sent me to live with my aunt."

"But you got curious about what happened to him?"

"That, and why he left the ranch to Blount. I guess the letter from my father, and the fact that Blount held me prisoner, will be enough to clear Jason as well as to get the will revoked."

"That'll make you owner of the biggest ranch in these parts," Rusty said. "You intend to stay here and live on it or go back east?"

"I've made up my mind to stay, but I'll need help with the ranch. Will you and Jason help me hire some good men once Ben Blount is no longer in control?"

"All you have to do is ask," Rusty said and smiled.

Jenny had finished eating when Jason rode in.

"Did you come across any sign?" Rusty asked.

"Nothing," Jason said.

"Well, I'm riding into town with you and Jenny just in case," Rusty declared.

"What about the herd, Rusty? After the sore head I gave Blount last night, if he rides in here looking for revenge and finds no one around, he's apt to run our herd off."

Rusty was silent for a moment, thinking. "Guess you're right," he said. "Reckon I better stay here."

"And keep your eyes open," Jason warned.

"You ever know me not to?"

"No."

"Then you just look to yourself and Miss Taylor," Rusty grumbled.

Chapter Thirteen

Darkness came long before Jason and Jenny reached New Castle. All signs of the recent storm had vanished, and the night was warm and friendly with the smell of sagebrush in the air. Overhead, innumerable stars graced an endless sky.

A few minutes later, they rode into town.

"I'm taking you straight to a friend of mine," Jason told Jenny as they reached the center of town.

Soon, he pulled up before an impressive house with well-tended grounds. Swinging from the saddle, he helped Jenny down. Together they walked along a path neatly bordered with flowers to the front door. Jason knocked and then stepped back.

"Who is it?" a woman's voice inquired from inside.

"Jason Ward."

The door was pulled inward an inch and a woman peered through the crack. She required a moment to recognize Jason in the darkness. When she did, she pulled the door wide open.

"What're you doing out so late, Jason Ward?" she scolded.

"I've brought you a boarder," Jason said. "Jenny Taylor, meet Mary Christian, the finest cook in the territory, and a friend of mine."

"Come in, Miss Taylor," Mary Christian said. "You've been the talk of the town of late. Has this rascal been treating you all right? Where did you find her, Jason?"

Mary Christian was heavyset and short, her height maybe five-feet-two or three. Her brown hair was streaked with gray and pulled loosely to a knot at the back of her head. Her round face was free of winkles, but the skin and the eyes suggested her age to be fifty or more. Despite the outward jollity and cheer, one sensed tragedy in those round features, as if something terribly sad had befallen her.

"She can tell you everything, Ma Christian," Jason said, using the name he had given Mary Christian out of affection. "Give her something to eat and a warm bed. If anyone other than the marshal or me comes looking for her, don't let them in. I'll see both of you in the morning."

Jason waited until they were both inside and he heard the lock turn. Then he walked to where the horses were tied. Climbing into the sorrel's saddle and leading the bay Jenny had ridden, he rode across town to Charlie Lambert's livery.

"You Charlie's boy?" he asked the freckle-faced kid who came out to meet him.

"Yes, sir. My name is Sammie."

"Sammie, give them a good rubdown and a feed of oats." Jason flipped the boy a silver dollar. "That's for you," he said. He flipped a second coin. "And that one is for the bill. I'll be back in a couple of hours. Have them saddled and ready. Can you do that?"

"Yes, sir. They'll be ready," the boy said with enthusiasm.

The marshal's office was locked, but Jason pounded on the door until he heard Boyd Gruber stirring inside.

"Better be something important," Gruber said, opening the door, six-gun in hand.

Jason pushed past him. "Got something I want you to read, Marshal," he said, and gave Gruber a piece of paper.

Marshal Gruber went to his desk, where a lamp burned dimly. Turning the wick up, he looked at Jason. "Now what's this that's so all-fired important you want me to read it?" he asked.

Jason gave him the envelope he'd been given by Jenny. Gruber opened it and began to read.

"Where did you get this?" Gruber demanded when he was finished.

"Have you met Jenny Taylor?" Jason asked.

"Met her! I've been searching the country over for her all day. Do you know where she is?"

"She's probably already in bed at Ma Christian's," Jason replied. "Blount was holding her prisoner, but I conked the guard over the head and got her out of the house through a window. She had found the letter in the house and gave it to me. Here it is."

"Why, that lying, no-good . . . I've got half a mind to go out there and . . . Blount told me he hadn't seen her!"

"You can take care of Blount later. Right now I want you to say you know I didn't kill Evan Taylor."

"Why?" Gruber asked, reading the letter. "This don't say Ben Blount killed Taylor. It just says Taylor was afraid of Blount. That don't undo the trial you went through nor the verdict of the jury. As far as I'm concerned, that case is still closed, and it'll take more than this to open it up again."

Jason could hardly believe Gruber's words. He reached for the letter, taking it from Gruber's hand. "Wasn't expecting you'd say that, Marshal," he said. Turning, he left the office, closing the door softly behind him.

A pale moon gave off little light as Jason walked to the home of Jim Tolbert, a big impressive house on the edge of town. He didn't know exactly what he intended to do, except somehow wrangle the truth from the banker.

A light was still burning when he stopped before the big house. The yard was surrounded by a white board fence about hip high, with a hitch rail in front. A low hedge ran along the outside of the fence as well. The house and surrounding flowers and shrubs obviously had had the best of care, better care than some people in New Castle, Jason decided.

He lifted the latch on the gate and walked along a path bordered by flowers in full bloom, but he was only dimly aware of the perfumed air that drifted up from the many blossoms. His knock brought heavy footsteps to the door, and suddenly, Jason stood face to face with Tolbert himself.

Tolbert stared at Jason a full moment before he spoke. "Ah . . . Mr. Ward, is it?" he asked, a bit nervously.

"I need to talk to you," Jason said.

"What about? Must be some kind of emergency for you to come to my home."

"Just bank business," Jason said.

"I don't talk bank business at my home," Tolbert said. "You'll have to see me when the bank opens in the morning."

He was too surprised to resist when Jason grabbed his belt and shoved him back inside the house. The room was well lit, and a lady with a lot of gray hair piled stylishly on top of her head sat on a settee to one side of a large fireplace. Her age was about forty, and she made a stately figure in a blue lace dress.

"Get him out of here, Jim!" she demanded in a high-pitched voice. "What does such a man mean forcing his way into our home like this?"

"Putting me out like that without hearing what I've come to say wouldn't be neighborly, ma'am," Jason said, pushing Tolbert into a chair. Standing threateningly over Tolbert, he said, "Now tell me about the will that gave the ET spread to Ben Blount! Did you help him write it?"

"That's none of your business, Ward," Tolbert replied, struggling once more for a banker tone and look.

"Ben Blount is a murderer and a crook, Tolbert. If you've got yourself mixed up in some scheme to cheat Jenny Taylor out of what's legally hers, you better get yourself free of it as fast as you can. The best way for you to do that is tell me what part you played in the scheme with Blount. Jenny Taylor found a letter from Evan Taylor. In that letter, Taylor says you were involved."

"I don't believe it. Show me that letter," Tolbert demanded.

Taking the letter from his pocket, Jason allowed Tolbert to read it. As he read, Tolbert's face drained of color. Jason could almost smell the man's fear.

"What is that letter about, Jim?" Mrs. Tolbert asked.

"Stay out of this, Minnie!" Tolbert ordered his wife, regaining a little confidence. "This man is a convicted murderer. He was released from Yuma Prison not six months ago."

"If he's a killer, you should get Marshal Gruber at once!" Minnie Tolbert exclaimed.

"I'll handle this myself," Tolbert replied, forcing some sternness into his voice. "Anyway, this is bank business. You go to bed, dear. I'll be up soon."

"If you're sure, husband."

"I'm sure. Good night, Minnie."

"Good night, husband," the lady replied, and disappeared into the back of the house.

The polite good nights struck Jason as bizarre under the circumstances.

"That will is perfectly legal, despite the letter," Tolbert said when his wife was gone. "When I tell the marshal how you forced your way in here, manhandling me in the process, you'll find your parole revoked."

Grasping Tolbert's shirt in one hand, Jason slapped the banker hard across his face.

Tolbert wilted completely after the slap. "Don't hit me again!" he pleaded, his face turning paler still.

"Are you ready to talk?" Jason asked.

"I already told you. . . ."

Jason slapped him again and threw him into a chair. The chair flew apart and left the banker sprawled on the floor amidst the rubble. Jason pulled him to his feet. Taking his knife from its sheaf, he pressed the point of the blade against Tolbert's fleshy neck.

"Talk or I'll slit your throat," Jason said menacingly.

"Don't cut me!" Tolbert pleaded. "I'll talk!"

"I'm listening."

"Ben Blount came to me with the plan. He said if I didn't help him he'd move the ET account from the bank. He said he'd see that other ranchers did the same. I'd have gone bust."

"Then you and Blount forged that will."

"Yes, but I had no choice. I think Blount would have killed me too, just like he did Taylor. You have to give me credit for something good, though."

"What's that?" asked Jason.

"I talked Blount into giving the girl twenty-five thousand

dollars. She would have been penniless without that money."

Jason let the banker fall to the floor. Tolbert lay on his back looking up at Jason, a disgusting, frightened man.

"Get up!" Jason ordered.

Tolbert, like a child fearful of punishment, scrambled to his feet.

"Now get a pen and some paper."

"What for?"

"You're going to write all that down and sign it," Jason said.

"No!"

Jason put the knife to his neck again and pressed the point against the skin. A drop of blood ran down the knife blade onto Tolbert's shirt.

"All right! Just don't cut me!" Tolbert managed to say, staring at the blood on the front of his shirt.

Tolbert went to a desk, sat down, wrote for a few minutes, then brought the paper to Jason. He had written essentially the same version of events he had related to Jason. Jason folded the paper and put it in his pocket along with the letter Evan Taylor had written.

"I'm going to see that every merchant in town and every rancher in the area sees Evan Taylor's letter and your confession," Jason told Tolbert. "I doubt they'll want a crook holding their money for them."

Jason left the banker standing in the middle of the room. The air outside had the fresh smell of the mountains, and Jason drew his lungs full to free himself of the stench of Jim Tolbert's slimy sweat. He walked down to the jail, intending to turn both letters over to Gruber. He tried the door but found it locked. A few minutes later, a sleepy-eyed man opened the door.

"Who are you?" Jason asked, not recognizing the man.

"Tom Dixon."

"Where's Marshal Gruber?"

"He had to go out of town," replied Dixon. "He hired me to sleep here and look after things."

"You live here in town?" Jason asked.

"I own the drugstore."

"When will Gruber be back?"

"In a couple of days. Is there something I can do for you?"

Jason felt like swearing. There was no man in town who'd buck Ben Blount without Gruber, even if he showed them the letters. Deciding he needed time to think, he headed for the livery. He would get the horses and ride back to the valley. Rusty would get a laugh out of the way Tolbert had folded.

Chapter Fourteen

There was little doubt in Ben Blount's mind that Jason Ward was the man who had knocked his man out and taken Jenny Taylor. He took a little time to consider what he should do, then he called Sky Smith into the foreman's room at the front of the bunkhouse.

"Get some men ready to ride," he ordered.

"How many riders you want, boss?" asked Smith.

"About ten, I guess," replied Blount.

"We going after Ward and the woman?"

"Yeah."

"You ask me, we don't need that many to take care of Ward and that old man," Smith said. "I'll ride out there and take care of both of them myself."

"You're always underestimating Ward!" Blount snapped. "Now get me ten of the best men we got in the bunkhouse and have them armed and ready to go at dark. And saddle my horse."

Blount stalked the room a couple of times as he went over the plan he had in mind. First, Jason and the old man would be killed. He'd save Jenny Taylor until he knew what her plan was to regain the ranch. If she wouldn't talk, he'd threaten to turn her over to the boys. That prospect would loosen any woman's tongue. When he was sure he had all the knowledge she possessed, he'd kill her himself and hide her body. Everyone would think she had wandered into the desert and died somewhere.

Hearing horses in front of the bunkhouse, he left the room and went outside, checking the load in his six-gun as he went. Smith tossed the reins of Blount's gelding to him, and Blount climbed aboard. His face grim, Blount led the men out of the ranch yard.

Blount pulled up when they reached the ridge looking down on Jason Ward's valley. A half moon had risen, but no lights showed from the camp beneath the cottonwood, and no one moved as far as Blount could see.

"We'll slip down to that tree and surround them. I want Ward and Hayes dead. Fill them full of lead, but if anyone shoots the woman, I'll feed his gizzard to the coyotes. Everyone understand that?"

There were hushed murmurs of understanding.

"Now follow me!" Blount ordered.

Fifty yards from the camp, Blount pulled up. "Spread out from here," he ordered, speaking barely above a whisper, "but I'll fire the first shot. After that, fill them full of lead."

At long last, he would be free of Jason Ward and the fear that the man would somehow prove his own innocence and show the world who had murdered Taylor on that fateful day.

He gave the men plenty of time to get into position. Then, six-gun in hand, he rode forward, the only sound the swish of his mount's hooves against the grass. A horse gave a whicker of greeting, and Blount knew the time had come.

A man came from a small tent and looked inquiringly around. "Now!" Blount yelled, and opened fire. Bullets from every direction poured into the camp. The man gave a yelp of pain and went down. Twisting and turning for a moment, he was then still.

"Hold your fire, men!" Blount shouted. "I think we got 'em all!"

Five minutes passed before Blount rode cautiously into the camp. Swinging from the saddle, he walked to the man and turned him over. "It's the only man!" he said, and then stooped and peered into the bullet-ridden tent. "Where in the hell is Ward? Get down and search for the scoundrel!" he ordered.

"Ain't no one else here," Smith said, emerging from the shadow of the cottonwood and coming to stand beside Blount. "We best ride out of here. No telling who might have heard those shots and will come riding in here to see what's happened."

Blount's frustration at missing Jason Ward was evident. Where was Ward? Obviously, he hadn't anticipated the raid against his camp, or he'd never have left the old man alone. Returning to Smith, he said, "Gather up the men, but we won't ride straight home. We'll ride north into the hills, laying down an obvious trail. When Ward returns, maybe he'll follow. If he does, we'll lay an ambush for him."

As Blount led his men north, he considered the consequences of killing Hayes. Ward would know who to blame for the murder. No one else had a reason. What would he do? Leave town and take Jenny Taylor with him? Hardly. Ward had suffered too much already. If Blount knew the man, the murder of the old man would set him off. Unease roiled momentarily in the pit of Blount's stomach.

* * *

When Jason heard the distant shots, he urged the sorrel into a gallop, fearful Blount and his men had paid the valley a visit and found Rusty alone.

The camp was strangely silent when Jason rode in. Where was Rusty? Surely not asleep after so much shooting. Pulling up near the tent, he looked around. Then he saw Rusty. Even in the faint moonlight there was no mistaking him. Jason swung from the saddle and knelt beside his old friend.

The old man was all shot up, but he was still alive. "Was it Blount, Rusty?" he asked.

"Him and maybe a dozen more," Rusty managed to get out.

"I'm sorry, Rusty. I should never have left you alone."

"Don't blame yourself, son," Rusty said, his voice barely a whisper, his breathing labored. "You couldn't let the girl ride into town by herself, and who knew Blount would come calling tonight. But make me a promise."

"Anything."

"Don't let Blount get away with all the wrong he's done."

"I'll swear to it, old pard," Jason whispered, as Rusty drew his last breath.

In death, Rusty Hayes looked sad and beaten. All the years of work and suffering showed in the old man's face. Despite the wounds, Jason slipped an arm beneath his shoulders, lifted the old man into his arms, and held him close for a moment.

"Rusty!" he whispered helplessly, tears filling his eyes. He would never sit across another campfire and listen to his old partner's tales of happenings long ago, never again hear him talk of the long ride from Tennessee. And he would never hear him tell again of Tobin Ward's bravery during the war.

Chapter Fifteen

Jason buried Rusty the next morning beneath the gnarled cottonwood, a spot Rusty was fond of. No one else was present, and that seemed appropriate to Jason, since they had been the one constant in each other's lives for so long.

As Jason stood over Rusty's grave, he had the feeling half his life was missing. He had loved Rusty as a friend, almost as a father, certainly as family. Remembering his promise, he swore he'd make Ben Blount and the men who rode with him wish they'd never heard the names Jason Ward and Rusty Hayes.

When he'd filled in Rusty's grave and rolled a stone into position to mark it, Jason, needing coffee at least, looked around for their supplies. What was left had been thoroughly trampled during the melee in which Rusty had been killed.

Saddling the sorrel, he rode out and checked the small herd of shorthorn first. Finding them grazing peacefully, he headed for New Castle to buy more supplies. He hoped Marshal Gruber had returned so he could report the raid. He'd also show Gruber Tolbert's confession. That should prove Blount's involvement even to Gruber.

His first stop was at the marshal's office. Tying the sorrel's reins about the hitch rail, he stooped beneath it and entered the office without knocking. Gruber sat behind his desk studying a set of Wanted posters.

"What can I do for you, Ward?" the marshal asked.

"Marshal, when I got home last night, my camp had been raided and Rusty shot full of holes."

"Dead?" asked Gruber.

"Not quite, but he died in my arms a few moments later."

"Did he say anything?" Gruber asked.

"He said the ranch had been raided by Ben Blount and maybe a dozen of his riders."

"Was he thinking straight?" asked Gruber.

"What kind of question is that?" Jason demanded, his anger rising.

"Just what I said. When a man's about dead, he may not be the best witness of what happened. Everybody knows you and Rusty consider Blount and the ET outfit your enemies. Rusty could have been mistaken. Naturally, I'll talk to Blount, but even if it was him and his riders, he's going to deny it. Without something further to go on, I'm afraid there's not much I can do."

"I thought a dying man's words meant a lot to the law," Jason protested.

"Look, Ward. I only got your word Rusty made such a dying declaration. For all I know right now, you could have shot Rusty yourself. Partners have been known to do that to each other."

"That is the most outlandish . . . !" Jason exploded in exasperation.

"You're an ex-convict, Ward. You've been convicted of murder already. Folks know that. They'll say a man who has killed once could kill again."

"I didn't kill Rusty, Marshal. He was like a father to me. I reckon I'll have to take care of his killers myself."

"Now you wait a minute, Ward!" Gruber said and stood up. "I told you I'd look into this. You start something before I find out what happened, you'll have me to deal with."

"Maybe these will help convince you Blount isn't on the level," Jason said, producing Jim Tolbert's confession.

Gruber read the confession before he said anything. Then he looked up at Jason. "This explains why Jim Tolbert resigned from the bank, sold his house, and left town," he said. "And I'll ride out and question Blount about it."

"When?"

"As soon as I have time."

Jason left the marshal's office frustrated at Gruber's seeming lack of concern. Climbing astride the sorrel, he rode down the street, stopping before the O.K. Saloon. Swinging down, he dropped the reins over the hitch rack, stepped up on the boardwalk, and went in, hoping he would see Blount or some of his riders. The place was empty except for the barkeep, Jake Bolton, and two wranglers Jason had never seen before.

"What'll you have?" Bolton asked, coming down the bar to Jason.

"Just looking for someone, Jake," Jason said, and turned back to the street. He was about to mount the sorrel when he heard someone call his name. Looking up the street, he saw Judge Blackburn walking toward him.

"Sorry about what happened to Rusty," the judge said.

"Thanks, Judge."

"I got a letter for you. Ben Richards in the post office asked me to give it to you. I told him if I didn't see you in a day or two I'd ride out to the ranch and deliver it myself. Heard a lot of talk about your valley. I'd like to see it."

"Thanks, Judge. You're welcome anytime."

"Stop in and see me anytime," Blackburn called over his shoulder as he headed to the courthouse.

The letter was from Mel Tenant and brought good news. Mel and Stacy McCauley were being paroled, and Mel reminded Jason of Jason's invitation for Mel and Stacy to visit. Jason had forgot about the letter he'd sent his friends telling them where they could find him. He glanced at the date at the top of the letter. They were probably well on their way here by now.

When Jason went to buy supplies, he stocked up appropriately, since he'd have two more mouths to feed. The imminent arrival of Mel and Stacy gave him something to think about other than Rusty's murder. He wondered how the two would react now to the trouble facing him. No doubt they'd want to lend a hand, but he'd had one friend killed already. He didn't want Mel and Stacy cut down by Blount and his men.

Jenny Taylor had never been far from his mind and, leaving the mercantile shop, Jason wondered if she was all right. Loading his supplies on behind the saddle, he swung onto the leather saddle and rode toward Ma Christian's house. The two were working in Ma Christian's flower garden when he rode up. They dropped hoes and gloves and met him at the gate.

"Bet you'd like a cup of coffee," Ma Christian greeted Jason.

"You bet I would."

"Jenny, you entertain this worthless fella on the front porch while I rustle up some coffee. I might even find a slice of raisin pie if I look hard enough."

"Are you and Ma getting along all right?" Jason asked when he and Jenny were seated on the porch. There was a smudge of dirt on her cheek, but Jason thought she looked beautiful.

"She mothers me something awful," Jenny replied. "I have to fuss at her before she'll let me do anything to help out around the place." She paused for a moment. "I heard the terrible news about Rusty, Jason. I know how close the two of you were. I feel like I'm somehow to blame."

"No one's to blame except Ben Blount and me," Jason replied.

Jenny was startled. "How could you be to blame?" she asked.

"I shouldn't have left him alone. If I'd been there, maybe I could have saved him. But you know how he was. Any hint he couldn't take care of himself left him furious. I don't reckon there'd have been a different outcome even if I'd been there. Rusty said Blount had a dozen men with him. He'd have killed us both."

"And both of you would be dead," Jenny added. She dropped her eyes, and a blush crept into her face.

Jason was puzzled. Had she said more than she intended and was now embarrassed that he might take what she'd said to mean more? *Or maybe . . .*

Ma Christian interrupted before Jason could finish the thought. "There," she said, offering Jason a tray on which sat three cups of steaming coffee and a slice of raisin pie. "The pie is yours, you handsome thing," she said to Jason as she passed a cup to Jenny, took one for herself, and sat in the nearby swing. "Eat up now," she commanded.

As saddened as he was by the loss of Rusty, Jason couldn't help but notice the beauty of the day as he rode home. Little did he realize that much of his pleasure came from the time he had spent with Jenny Taylor.

Most men who had spent time in prison would be inclined to appreciate such a day, he thought to himself. Tiny, shy wildflowers of various colors, sizes, and shapes bordered the sides of the trail. Even the cactus looked greener and the wind carried the subtle smells of the desert. But soon the sun would heat everything up and the country would take on its usual character.

Jason's first and foremost impulse after seeing Marshal Gruber was to head for the Taylor ranch and inflict as much damage as he could. The only thing that held him back was the sure knowledge that he wouldn't last long in a face-to-face fight with the whole crew, and this was one fight he must win, for Rusty's sake.

He had to plan each move carefully so, when the fight was over, he would not only survive, but the blame would point to Blount. The thing to do, he decided, was to provoke Blount into attacking the valley again. When he came, Jason would be ready.

Jason chose another sheltered spot beneath a different cottonwood for a campsite. Fallen trees on either side formed a barrier a man would have trouble climbing through without making noise. Immediately behind the site, the bank of the stream dropped straight down for several feet. The bank was slick and would be difficult to climb and, hopefully, a man wouldn't be able to do it silently. That left only the front open, and Jason rolled a line of boulders into place there, stacking smaller boulders on top of larger, forming a barrier behind which he could fight if and when Blount attacked.

Figuring he was as prepared as he would ever be, Jason decided to put the first step of his plan into action that night. Meanwhile, he set about preparing his supper as usual. He built a small fire, brought water from the stream, and set it near the fire to boil. Next, he sliced some bacon into a frying pan, let it begin to cook, and then peeled a couple of potatoes, sliced them, and stirred them in with the bacon. The bacon grease would season the potatoes. When the water was boiling, he added coffee. A few minutes later, he sat on a stone he had rolled in for a seat and ate his supper.

A little after twilight, and with the fire burned down, he brought the sorrel into the camp and saddled him, leaving him nearby till the time came for him to ride for the Taylor spread. Sitting with his back to the cottonwood, he went over his plan again.

The moon rose about ten and, keeping in the shadows along the stream, he held the sorrel to a walk. When he left the valley, he put the sorrel into a canter, which would get him to his destination well after everyone was in bed.

No lights showed in any of the buildings when Jason arrived. Taking a position in the scrubby oaks overlooking the ranch house, he draped the sorrel's reins over a limb, leaving them untied. If he was in a rush when he returned, he wouldn't have time to undo a knot. Then he took the bag of supplies he had brought with him from the saddlebags.

When the next cloud passed over the moon, Jason took advantage of the darkness and quickly worked his way down the slight hillside, passing through clumps of prickly pear and a few cholla cacti, whose shapes looked like emaciated bodies in the pale light.

When he reached the clearing, he dropped to his knees and studied the buildings again. The barns and corrals, as well as the house, were too far away for him to get to all of them easily, but the long bunkhouse was no more than fifty yards to his right.

The bunkhouse then would be his target, but the distance would have to be crossed without benefit of cover. He waited patiently for another cloud to cover the moon. Then he dashed to the corner of the bunkhouse. He paused for a moment, pressed himself as close to the building as possible, and regained his wind. Then he crept slowly along the building and around a corner to the rear.

Once there, he opened the bag, removed a small bottle of kerosene, and splashed the oil over the bunkhouse wall. Striking a match, he set the oil on fire. Then he ran as fast as he could back the way he had come.

When he reached the sorrel, the horse's ears were cast forward, and he was nervously eyeing the growing flames below. "Never mind, old boy, that fire ain't gonna come all the way up here," Jason assured him. Pulling the Winchester from its sleeve, he waited until the first men burst from the bunkhouse and squeezed off the first shot.

The front man tumbled forward and lay still. He brought another man down with his second shot before anyone realized what was happening. Before he could get off a third, the rest of the men made a wild dash toward either the house or the barn. Meanwhile, the flames from the burning bunkhouse soared into the night, casting jumping shadows across the ranch-house yard.

Ramming the Winchester into his saddle boot, Jason climbed aboard the sorrel and quietly rode west and out of the valley. Later, he turned into the hills and worked his way back to his own ranch.

He took no pleasure in the fact that he had killed the men, though they were killers themselves. They had laid down the rules when they killed Rusty. When a man faced an enemy without principle, he couldn't play by conventional rules and stay alive, and Jason felt no regret at retaliating in the same way.

Indeed, there was no other way he could retaliate. He either had to kill some of Blount's men or scare them off if he was to even the odds.

Chapter Sixteen

Sunshine filtering through the leaves overhead hit Jason's face and woke him. He lay still for a moment, hearing only the sounds of nature. Sitting up, he looked around. His movement startled a couple of mockingbirds overhead in the limbs of the cottonwood. The birds quarreled angrily as they fluttered higher into the tree.

The sorrel had clipped a clean circle in the grass around his stake pin and, knowing the horse needed water, Jason reached for his boots, shook them out, and pulled them on. Strapping the Peacemaker around his waist, he walked out to the horse and led him to water.

The sorrel suddenly lifted his head, threw his small ears forward, and stared at the ridge above. Following the horse's gaze, Jason saw four riders top the ridge and head down the slope. At the bottom of the slope, they pulled up and looked around.

Jason hurried back into camp for the Winchester and watched the riders approach. With relief, he recognized the slim form of Mel Tenant and the lankier Stacy McCauley. Another man was Tee Martin. As far as he could tell from a distance, Jason had never seen the fourth man before.

The riders pulled up, and Mel and Stacy dropped to the ground and rushed to greet Jason. After there were hand-shakes all around, Stacy introduced the fourth rider.

"Meet my Uncle Barney, Jason. He came down to Yuma to see me. I brought him along."

Barney McCauley was pretty much an older version of Stacy. He had an open, honest look, and Jason liked him immediately. "You're welcome, Mr. McCauley," he said and shook the elderly man's hand.

"I'd appreciate it if you called me Barney."

"Guess you know this one," Mel said, indicating Tee Martin.

"What're you doing out here, Tee?" Jason asked.

"Heard what you been doing for Miss Taylor," Tee replied. "You're bucking some big odds. I thought I might even them a little."

"You couldn't be more welcome," Jason answered, "but the bullets that'll be flying around here are for real. You oughta remember that."

"I've faced bullets before," Tee replied gruffly.

"What's been going on around here?" asked Stacy, noting the destruction.

"Some of the natives aren't so friendly," Jason said. "They raided the valley last night and killed Rusty."

"Tee told us all about your trouble, and the cause of it," replied Stacy. "What I can't figure out is why you haven't already hit back."

"I paid Blount a visit last night, but we won't talk about that now. The four of you must be hungry. I'll cook us up some grub."

"Show me the fixings," Barney said. "I'll do the cooking as long as I hang around."

"I wouldn't hear of it," Jason protested.

"He's a stubborn old cuss, Jason," Stacy said and

laughed. "Claims he can't stand anybody's cooking but his own."

"Well, I wouldn't want to hurt his feelings," Jason said and smiled.

"I'll find everything I need," Barney said. "You boys settle down and visit."

"Together we'll settle this fellow Blount's hash," Mel said.

"No, I don't want to involve you fellows in this fight. I've already lost one friend. I don't want to lose any more."

"We came down here to ride for you, Jason," Mel replied. "Guess our getting involved is up to us. You agree, Stacy?"

"I couldn't agree more," Stacy said. "What kind of hands would we be if we didn't stand up for the brand?"

"Count me in," Barney called from the fire.

"And me too," Tee said.

Jason looked at each in turn. "As of now you're all on the payroll," he said, his affection for the foursome showing in his face and voice. "But I should warn you. I'm expecting Blount and his men to hit back anytime. So keep your guns handy and your eyes and ears open."

"We'll keep our eyes peeled," Mel said. The others agreed.

Jason remained uneasy about their decision, however. He wasn't sure his friends knew how dangerous the situation was.

They began the job of rebuilding the next morning. Stacy and Mel went to the stand of trees near the end of the valley and began cutting poles for a corral. Barney and Jason stayed behind to discuss how the cabin should be built.

"You ever consider adobe?" Barney asked. "Hard to burn adobe with a sod roof."

"I don't know anything about adobe," Jason said.

"Happens I do. If we can find a supply of the right kind of clay around here, I'll build it for you. Be cooler in summer and warmer in winter."

"That's fine with me," Jason replied, "and I'll work with you."

"I'll ride out and look the valley over," Barney said. "I expect I'll find what we need."

Jason busied himself marking off the approximate dimensions of the house he had in mind. When he was finished, he made a pot of fresh coffee, sat on a rock, and sipped the dark liquid while he waited for Barney to return.

"I found plenty," Barney said when he returned. "Plenty of everything we'll need at the bottom of that slope a hundred yards off. Mel and Stacy can furnish us with the poles and logs we'll need, and we'll need lumber for walls and ceilings, else everything inside will get a full share of grit."

"I'll ride into town and pick some up," Jason told him.

Leaving the house entirely in Barney's hands, Jason rode into New Castle for the lumber. When he went to the livery to rent a wagon, Charlie Lambert offered to sell him one with a team of mules at a good price.

"Though I'll be happy to keep taking your money in rent, you'll always have need of a wagon out there," Lambert urged.

"You're right, Charlie. I do need a wagon and team, but I think I'd rather have mules for the wagon. You got two good mules?"

"The best around. Come with me and I'll show you."

Lambert led two red mules with black trim from their stalls. "Take a look," Lambert said. "From Missouri and they're well broke."

"How old are they?" Jason asked.

"About four, I'd say."

Jason walked to the head of the first mule, took the upper lip in one hand, the lower in the other hand, and parted the mule's lips. After studying the teeth of the first mule a moment, he did the same with the second. "Looks about the right age," he said. When the price was agreed upon, Jason hitched the mules to the wagon, tied the sorrel behind, and went to the hardware store for the lumber. As he passed the blacksmith shop, Sam Blankenship stopped him and reminded him he still had to pick up the branding iron.

"I need a supply of nails too," Jason told him.

"Got plenty. What size?"

"Ten pounds of eight penny and a pound of tens should do it," Jason said, and waited as Lambert weighed and sacked the nails. When Lambert was finished, Jason paid him for both the branding iron and the nails.

On his way out of town, Jason stayed alert for any sign of Blount or his men. A man in a slow wagon was easier pickings than some on a fast horse, and Jason was expecting Blount to strike back anytime, but nothing happened.

When the corral was finished, Stacy helped Uncle Barney with the house while Mel joined Tee in rebuilding the barn. Jason was surprised at how fast the work went. He was also surprised that a day had passed and Blount had yet to attack.

"Maybe he knows you're no longer alone here and he don't want to take on five of the roughest hombres in the territory," Stacy suggested with a smile when Jason brought the subject up.

"Maybe, but Blount has twenty men at his disposal," Jason replied. "I don't know what's holding him back, but we can't allow ourselves to get careless."

"What if he don't come?" asked Stacy.

"Then I'll go after him again when the time is right," Jason replied.

"Remember me telling you how selfish he was," Mel joked. "Wants all the fun for himself. He was like that every time we had a run-in in Yuma. Always insisting on tackling the toughest hombre alone."

"Just plum selfish," added Stacy.

The sorrel woke Jason with a whicker that night. Recognizing the horse's welcome when spotting another of his kind, Jason quickly woke the others. "If any of you don't want to be a part of this fight," he said when they were awake, "you better ride out now."

"You think Blount's about to return your raid?" Mel asked.

"Somebody's out there." Taking the Winchester, Jason eased out to the line of boulders.

Barney came and knelt beside him. "Everyone's all set. You see anything?"

Before Jason could answer, a rifle exploded no more than fifty yards out, and a bullet splattered a nearby boulder. That first shot was the signal for the all-out attack. Now a dozen riders swarmed in from three sides, guns blazing, leaving Jason and his men hemmed up against the stream.

Jason took aim at a rider and squeezed off a shot. The horse went down, letting out a squeal that reverberated around the valley as the rider was pitched forward. Neither horse nor rider moved after that. Other horses went down and, from somewhere in the darkness, there came a shouted order for the attackers to dismount and attack on foot.

Now there was less commotion, but the firing continued as the line before the campsite slowly advanced, the flashes pushing the darkness aside briefly as guns exploded and bullets pelted the boulders, the fallen trees, and the limbs of the cottonwood. By then, the smell of burnt powder was heavy.

As the attackers advanced from the front, the rest of the men joined Jason and Barney behind the boulders and kept up a heavy fire that slowed the advance. A slug sang eerily off the boulder in front of Jason and careened off into the night. Then, as suddenly as the attack began, it ended.

In the absence of gunfire, Jason heard the groans of both men and horses. The sounds were pitiful, especially those of the horses, but the likelihood that some of Blount's gunmen still lurked in the darkness was too great for anyone to go put the horses out of their misery.

"Everyone all right?" Jason asked.

"Fine," Mel said.

"Me too," Stacy said.

"Tee?"

"I'm fine."

"Barney?"

When he got no answer from Barney, Jason reached a hand out to him. Barney didn't move, and then Jason's hand found something wet and warm. Bending low behind the boulders, he struck a match and held it to Barney's face. There was no mistaking the vacant look in his eyes. Jason brought his hand gently down on them, closing them once and for all.

"Barney's dead, boys," he said softly.

Stacy walked over and knelt silently by his uncle. The only sound of grief was an expressive deepening of his breath.

"I'm awfully sorry, Stacy," Jason said. "He worked hard on the house, and now he won't get to enjoy it. I guess I should never have hired him on, knowing the danger he'd be in."

Stacy rose. "You couldn't have run him off, Jason. He knew of our friendship in prison."

"Another reason to go after Blount if he ain't lying

out there already dead," Mel said. "The only solution is to shoot Blount, and I hope I'm the one who gets to do it."

Jason was fairly sure they would hear no more from Blount and his gang that night. Still, taking the Winchester and keeping to the shadows, he made a circle around the camp. He came upon both dead horses and men, but found no one alive. He had come to know the night sounds of the valley and, hearing nothing that didn't belong there, he crept back to camp.

By the time he returned, the eastern rim of the horizon was sprouting some light. While he was out, Mel and Stacy had wrapped Barney in a blanket and tied it off.

"I thought I would bury him beneath that tree near Rusty, if you've no objections," Stacy said.

"Rusty and I both would be honored to have Barney rest there," Jason told him. "They were a lot alike, you know, and I'll pay homage to both each time I visit their graves."

Jason made a small fire, put water for coffee on to boil, and cooked up bacon and flapjacks. They ate, though no one demonstrated much of an appetite. When they were finished, Stacy took a shovel and went to the cottonwood. Mel volunteered to wash the dishes, and a little later they laid Barney to rest near Rusty.

"What'll we do with them?" Mel asked, indicated the dead horses and men in front of the camp.

"I don't want them buried in the valley," Jason said.

"Be quite a job hauling them out," replied Stacy.

"We'll make the effort," Jason told them. "Stacy, you hitch up the mules and load the dead men into the wagon. Mel and I will saddle up and drag the horses out."

Remembering a deep wash beyond the valley, Jason dragged a horse there and rolled him in. Piling horses and men on top of each other, they then crushed the banks of the wash down, covering the combined pile of dead.

"A pity good horses have to lie for all time with that bunch of garbage," Mel observed solemnly when the work was finished.

"Stacy, can you finish the work on the house alone?" Jason asked the next day, having taken the rest of the previous day off out of respect for Barney.

"Ain't much else to do," Stacy said. "Just a little touching up. We can move in anytime, but what're we going to do for furniture?"

"How would you and Mel like to hitch up the wagon, go into town, and pick us up some basics? A stove, a table and some chairs, and some ticking for a few mattresses?"

"I can make all the chairs we need," Stacy said. "I took a job working in the prison shop after you left Yuma. I helped make chairs for the warden's den. They turned out all right."

"That's fine with me," Jason replied.

"Wish we had feathers to go in them mattresses," Mel said. "Be a lot softer than grass and wouldn't rattle when a body turned on them."

"Guess hay will have to do, since we don't have anything around here to pluck," Jason countered.

"What else do we need?" Stacy asked.

"Anything you think we can't do without," Jason said. "But I'd like a promise from both of you. If you run into Blount or any of his men, go out of your way to keep out of a fight. I've got some plans in mind, and I'll need the both of you to help me carry them out."

"Reckon I'll ride in with them," Tee said. "I expect they been expecting me to make another run. Anything I can tell Miss Jenny, Jason?" he asked.

Jason could think of a lot of things he'd like her to know, for her image had been constantly in his mind. But when the time came, if it ever did, he hoped he could say them himself.

After they were gone, Jason saddled the sorrel and rode out to check the cattle. They were far too contented on the thick grass and nearby shade to wander out of the valley. Still, he felt better making sure.

As he rode back to the camp, he saw a lone rider top the ridge. Pulling the sorrel up, he reached for the Winchester, laid it across his saddle, and sat watching the rider come in. He was both shocked and pleased when he recognized Jenny Taylor.

"Miss Taylor," he said when she pulled her horse up before him.

"I thought we agreed on Jenny and Jason," she replied and smiled.

"Jenny, then."

"Ben Blount sent a couple of riders into town to be doctored for bullet wounds. The talk around town is that he and his men called on you. I came out to see if you were all right."

"Barney McCauley, one of my riders, was killed. With the exception of Barney, though, we're fine."

"I'm sorry about your man," she said. "Is there anything I can do before I go back to town?"

"You can let me give you a cup of coffee."

"I'd like that," she said, smiling.

Jason helped her dismount, very conscious of the warmth of her hand when he held it.

"I see you've begun to build," Jenny said as they walked into the camp. "I like an adobe house. I hear they're cool in summer and warm in winter."

"We haven't moved in yet, but Mel and Stacy left some time ago to buy furniture. I'm surprised you didn't meet them."

"I did, and Tee was with them. We visited for a few minutes, and they drove on. Is that Rusty's grave I saw over there beneath the cottonwood?" she asked gently.

"Rusty's and Barney's. Barney was the man they killed last night. He was Stacy's uncle."

Jenny sat on a rock beneath the cottonwood while Jason stirred a handful of dried leaves into the coals of the morning fire. When the leaves caught, he piled on some twigs, took the coffeepot to the stream, and filled it. Adding a few larger pieces to the fire, he put the water on to boil and went to sit near Jenny.

"How long were you in prison?" she suddenly asked.

"Five years. I was paroled when I was eligible."

"I expect you must be bitter after losing five years of your life like that."

"Not so much about being in prison," Jason said. "I made some good friends there. But I'm bitter about the fact that Blount did the killing and has never been made to pay."

The water had begun to boil, and Jason went to the fire and emptied some fresh grounds into the pot. Setting the pot a little back from the fire to let the coffee brew, he then found cups. Filling the cups, he carried them to where Jenny waited.

"Smells good," she said, taking the cup offered her.

"I hope it tastes that way," Jason said.

She took a sip. "Perfect."

Jason was pleased, though he suspected she might be indulging in a little social fib, since the look on her face failed to reflect the satisfaction with which she spoke.

"I have a favor to ask," she said after a moment.

"You have only to tell me."

"Judge Blackburn has offered to look into my father's will. He intended to talk with Mr. Tolbert about it but Tolbert has left town. Sold out his interest in the bank and left without saying where he was going. His sudden departure was a puzzle to everyone."

"I expect New Castle will be a better town," Jason said. "But what's the favor?"

"I want to come out here and live. I have nothing to keep me busy in town, and there is much I could do here. You need a cook, and I'll work until everything about my place is settled. How about it?"

For a moment, Jason was too stunned to speak. "You haven't thought this through thoroughly," he finally said. "We're three ex-convicts. What would people in town think and say if you came out here and lived with us?"

"I've thought about that, and I don't care. I told the judge and Mrs. Christian. They disapprove and tried to talk me out of it, but not because they were worried that something would happen to me. They thought such a move lacked propriety on my part, but I've made up my mind . . . That is, if you agree."

"I agree with the judge and Mrs. Christian. And there's something else as well," Jason said.

"What?" asked Jenny.

"You would be in danger. Blount means to kill me. He'll make a raid on the valley again soon enough. When he does, I wouldn't want you here. He wouldn't leave any witnesses behind. Your being a woman would make no difference to him."

"I can take care of myself," Jenny replied with spirit. "I can shoot and I can ride. When they come, I'll help defend the place."

Jason didn't know what to say but, secretly, he was pleased that she trusted him so much.

"Do you agree that I can come out here?" she asked again.

"When Blount finds out you're here, he'll want you dead as much as he does me. Have you thought of that?"

"But we have joined forces, haven't we?"

"I guess so."

She smiled. "I brought a few things with me, enough to do me until I can get back into town and pick up more. Now, where do I begin?"

"When Stacy and Mel get back, you can help them get the house in shape. You'll live in the adobe. Stacy, Mel, and I will eat inside, but we'll sleep in the barn."

"Or outdoors, like you've been doing," she said, looking at the bedrolls surrounding them.

"Well, there's something to be said for seeing the stars at night when you've been locked up for five years."

She leaned closer and put a hand on his arm. "Thanks, Jason. You've done a lot for me. I only hope sometime I can do as much for you."

She removed her hand and stepped away, but even with her hand no longer there, Jason could still feel its warmth.

Chapter Seventeen

Life in the valley took on a different feel after Jenny came. Mel and Stacy found all sorts of excuses to hang around the house, ready to come to blows over who would bring water from the spring or wood for the stove.

"When do we go after Blount?" Stacy asked one evening as the three men sat in front of the house.

"How about tomorrow?" Jason asked, surprising the other two.

"What're we gonna do?" Mel wanted to know.

"First, there's something we ought to settle. We can't ever leave Jenny alone. One of us must always be near."

"That's gospel," agreed Stacy.

"We can't hit Blount and his men head-on," Jason said, "but there are ways. Folks say the Apache Indians are maybe the greatest fighters ever. You know how they fight?"

"Hit and run," Stacey said.

"That's what we'll do. We'll hit them every chance we get, then we'll run. If we can take out a few more riders, maybe the others will decide that sticking with Blount is

116

too risky. But one thing we all have to remember: Blount's tough and smart. He'll take advantage of every mistake we make."

"Who'll ride with you tomorrow, me or Mel?" Stacy asked.

"Mel. You stay with Jenny."

Jason and Mel reached the Taylor spread just past noon, tied their mounts, and took a position in the oaks overlooking the ranch house. The sun was at its hottest, and the oaks, thin limbed and small leafed, provided little shade.

Jason saw no movement around the place, but a half-dozen saddled horses were tied up at the hitch rail before a new bunkhouse.

"You stay here," Jason said. "I'm going to slip down closer and put a couple of shots into that new bunkhouse. When they come out, I'll try for the leaders."

"Why can't I go down with you?" Mel asked.

"They'll come boiling out of that bunkhouse, hit the saddle, and be after me before I get back up the hill. That'll be your cue. Knock as many as you can from the saddle. That'll give me a chance to make it back up the hill."

"All right, if that's the way you want it," Mel agreed reluctantly.

The heat seemed to increase as Jason made his way down the hillside. Lizards and scorpions, huddling in what shade they could find, scattered before him. Deciding he was close enough, he flipped a tarantula spider as big as his hand out of the way and went to his belly. Bringing the rifle into position, he took aim and fired two rapid shots into the small bunkhouse window. A few moments later, a bullet smacked the ground near him, the explosion coming from the direction of the house.

Two more bullets splashed dirt over him before he was

in position to see Blount standing before the house with smoke trailing from the rifle he held in his hands.

Now men were rushing out of the bunkhouse. Two quick shots from the Winchester sent all but one scurrying back inside. The one left behind was dragging himself toward the bunkhouse door.

Only winged one man, Jason thought to himself, and cursed silently at the missed opportunity.

Jason's shots into the men had taken only a fraction of a second. Meanwhile, Blount had continued firing from the front of the house. Turning his rifle on Blount, Jason sent a couple of shots in his direction, missing with both. He knew he had to do something and do it quickly before the men from the bunkhouse joined the fight. He took careful aim at Blount and squeezed off a shot just as Blount turned. Jason's bullet hit the door behind him. Blount, recognizing how close the bullet had come, shoved the door open and disappeared inside.

The man Jason had hit made it halfway through the door and collapsed. Jason figured he was dead and, deciding he had inflicted as much damage as he could, started back up the hill.

The men inside the bunkhouse must have seen him, for some ventured out again and began firing at him as he climbed the hill. Two men ran for their horses, mounted, and charged the hill after Jason. Mel opened fire from the top of the hill, turning the riders back.

Jason was out of wind when he reached the hilltop. He threw himself down beside Mel. Through the open doorway of the house, Blount was ordering his men to continue the fight.

Men shooting uphill are already at a disadvantage. Men shooting uphill from the back of a running horse are doubly so. That thought must have hit Blount's men at about the same time for, suddenly, they headed in the opposite direction.

Mel and Jason made their way to their mounts, climbed up, and rode out, taking a northern direction toward some badlands. Before reaching those, if Blount didn't pursue them, they'd circle back toward home. If Blount gave chase, they would hole up in one of the numerous canyons. After a few miles, they pulled up and studied their back trail.

"Ain't no dust back there," Mel observed.

A horrendous thought suddenly raced through Jason's mind. "What if Blount went straight to the valley instead of chasing us? he said.

"Then we better get there first," Mel replied.

Both men were much relieved to find all was well when they arrived back in the valley.

Chapter Eighteen

Jason knew Blount would strike back. The only question was when, and they had to be ready, which meant having a man on watch twenty-four hours a day. Jason decided they'd pull eight-hour watches—eight on and sixteen off. He broached the subject to Mel and Stacy, and they agreed.

"I'll take a turn too," Jenny said, overhearing their talk.

The three men objected, but Jenny insisted, arguing she could watch and listen as well as they could. Finally, the men agreed, and they pulled straws to see who took the first watch. Jenny drew the shortest straw. Jason would relieve her later in the night.

When Jenny woke him, he strapped the Peacemaker on and, taking the Winchester with him, found a rock well out from the buildings and sat down, the rifle across his knees. The silence was foreboding, as if the night life sensed danger, but the star-studded heavens seemed to deny the existence of any such thing.

As the night wore on, the moon made its arc across the northern sky and then began to pale. A wind rose, rustling the grass and stirring the leaves of the cottonwoods.

"Jason?

Stirred from his thoughts by the call, Jason turned and saw Jenny a few feet behind him. "You should be asleep," he said. "We got a full day tomorrow."

"I was in bed, but I couldn't sleep," she replied, taking a seat beside him.

She was close enough that her elbow brushed his arm, and he caught the faint odor of the gardenia perfume she favored.

"You think they'll come anytime soon?" she asked.

"Yes, but we won't be here."

"Where will we be?

"I've been thinking. Maybe we should set a trap for Blount," he told her. "See that ridge up there?"

"Yes."

"Come early morning, we'll settle you in there with a horse and some supplies. Mel, Stacy, and I will be further down. When Blount comes, we'll let him and his men ride in. When they fail to find us, they'll probably decide to burn everything. Before they can do that, we'll cut down on them from our cover."

"What if that fails?" Jenny asked. "What if they attack you? Blount will have a lot of men with him."

"We'll have mounts nearby. If they come close to over-running our positions, we'll run like scared rabbits. If they do seem to be getting the best of us, you mount that horse and head for New Castle and Judge Blackburn as fast as you can."

"I'll say a prayer," she said.

"I'm not sure the Lord will appreciate being brought into this mess, but you can try Him."

Jenny stood. "Well, if I'm going to be living in the rocks up there tomorrow, I had better go in and put a few things together." Lowering her head, she kissed Jason gently on his cheek. "That's for luck," she said, and Jason, too startled to say anything, listened to her retreating footsteps.

He passed the few hours until it was time to wake Stacy a little confused. He told himself that such a kiss was nothing more than a gesture of appreciation on Jenny's part. When the time came, Jason went to the barn and woke Stacy and Mel. Before Stacy went out to stand watch, he explained his plan for the next day.

"That sounds like you think Blount might be coming today," Mel said.

"I don't know if he'll come today or not," Jason replied. "But he'll come."

In the distance, a flash of lightning split the sky, followed by a low roll of thunder.

Jason woke at mid-morning to the smell of brewed coffee. He drank a cup and walked out to select the places from which the three men would wait the coming of Blount and his men. When he came back in, Jenny had made flapjacks, and the four of them ate together.

"Saddle mounts for all of us, including Jenny," he told Stacy and Mel when they were finished eating. "I've selected the spots where we'll lie in wait. If there is any danger they'll overrun us, remember, we're to ride out of here like scalded cats."

"What about these dishes?" Jenny asked.

"Leave them. I want everyone in place right away."

Jason followed Jenny to her place on the ridge to make sure she was safely hidden. "Your mount will be out of sight up here," he said, "but if you want to watch you can get behind the boulders to the front there."

Jenny rode into the rocks. When she returned on foot, she carried her rifle.

"I'd rather they didn't see any shooting coming from up here," Jason said.

"Just in case," Jenny replied.

Their eyes met and Jason felt something pass between them. He wanted to say something, but he couldn't think of any words to express what he was feeling. He wasn't even sure he understood it.

"Be careful and stay well hidden," he said.

"And you be careful," Jenny replied.

Turning the sorrel about, Jason rode to his own place of concealment further down the slope.

Chapter Nineteen

Jason carefully studied the different places of concealment in which he had placed Mel and Stacy, making sure
neither could be seen. Then he lay back and tried to relax,
his thoughts more on Jenny than the ambush he had set.

The morning began hot, and the heat increased as the
sun rose higher. There was no wind to move the stifling
weight that hung over the valley like an invisible shroud.

Jason's shirt was soaked, and drops of warm sweat ran
down his face and into his eyes. He thought of the others
and knew they were suffering. He was on the point of calling the whole thing off when he saw a rider appear in the
entrance of the valley from the direction of the Taylor
ranch.

Jason watched for a moment and, when no one else appeared, decided the rider might be some drifter riding in
for a meal. Then movement pulled his attention to the other
entrance, and he saw two riders there. Others appeared behind them, at least a half a dozen. Turning back to the
opposite entrance again, he saw more riders there, more

than a dozen in all. Blount had hemmed them in and meant to see that no one escaped the valley.

At some unseen signal, the riders began to move in from both ends. Jason watched as they converged, seeing at once that one bunch would ride squarely into and over the places where Stacy and Mel were hidden. They would flush Mel and Stacy from hiding like bird dogs given the command to flush quail.

He tried desperately to think of something he could do to help them, but everything that came to mind meant exposing his own position. *If it comes down to that,* he told himself, *you'll have no choice but to do it.* But Mel and Stacy, spotting the approaching riders, opened fire.

Jason saw two riders go down. Others, caught unaware, pulled up and sought to locate the source of the attack. Then they began to close in on the shallow ravine where Mel and Stacy were hidden.

Jason swung into the sorrel's saddle and raced to the rescue of his friends. When Blount's men saw Jason, they turned their guns on him. He heard the hot whine of a bullet whistle past his head. Another clipped the horn of his saddle and caterwauled away. Then something clutched at his left arm, burning like the sting of an angry wasp.

Bringing the Winchester up, Jason put bullet after bullet into the midst of the riders, hoping to break the circle closing in on Stacy and Mel. A horse went down. A moment later, another rider was knocked from the saddle, whether by a bullet from his gun or Stacy's and Mel's, Jason had no idea. Then the charge of the riders broke and, turning, they rode hard back toward the entrance of the valley.

Pulling the sorrel up, Jason took careful aim at the back of the nearest rider, squeezed the trigger, and missed. Hearing firing from behind, he turned, expecting to see some of

Blount's men coming from that direction. Instead, he saw that Jenny had left the boulders and was racing toward him, firing at riders coming in from his left. With a prayer for Stacy and Mel, Jason turned back, raked the sorrel's sides, and rode to meet Jenny.

"Why didn't you stay hidden?" he yelled angrily, pulling up alongside her.

"You want me to stay up there and watch the rest of you get killed?" she shouted back.

"Follow me!" Jason yelled and, turning the sorrel about, headed back up the slope to the boulders.

"What about Stacy and Mel?" she yelled from behind him.

Looking back, he saw she had made no move to follow. *Confounded, stubborn woman!* he said to himself and, turning back, grabbed her mount's reins and headed again for the boulders. When they were almost there, he dropped back and gave Jenny's bay a hard whack with the Winchester, sending him into the boulders.

"Now stay there!" he yelled, and turned back to the fight below.

Someone from the valley shouted an order, and the guns went silent. What the cease-fire portended, Jason had no idea, but he slid from the sorrel's saddle and took up a position behind a boulder. As he waited, he remembered he had seen nothing of Blount thus far. His eyes roamed the valley, but Blount was nowhere to be seen, nor was the big gray horse Blount had ridden of late.

Down below, a man Jason recognized as Sky Smith gathered his men about him. Jason could hear nothing of what he was saying, but from his gestures he was passing out orders, possibly preparing to begin the attack on Mel and Stacy again.

Only moments before, the valley had seemed a hellish

place of fire and brimstone, and that impression was enforced now by the clouds of gun smoke that rose in the air, accompanied by the overwhelming smell of burnt powder.

The silence held and Jason continued to study the distance to the ravine where Mel and Stacy lay hidden. Should he try to make it down there and join them? He eyed the distance—at least a couple hundred yards, maybe more, with only an intermittent boulder in between for cover. His chances of covering the distance without being seen were remote. Suddenly, he heard a scream from behind. Turning, he saw Jenny run from the boulders with a man in hard pursuit. Ben Blount! The mystery of the big man's absence on the battlefield was solved.

Blount had been somewhere over the ridge beyond the boulders, and he now held Jenny, who was kicking and screaming, fighting him with all her might. Then Jason saw Blount raise his hand and bring it down hard on her jaw, and Jenny fell limp in his arms.

Jason let loose a yell of rage that left his throat raw, and ran as fast as he could back to the ridge as Blount, still holding Jenny, disappeared into the boulders. Before Jason hit the rocks, he heard the sound of a horse running hard. Dashing through the boulders, he was just in time to see Blount on the gray, with Jenny in front of him, heading north at a hard run.

Jason raced to where he had left the sorrel. As he climbed into the saddle, something with the force of a mule kick hit him. Jason was knocked backward and lay unmoving on the ground beneath the sorrel's hooves.

Chapter Twenty

Jason seemed to be swimming in darkness toward some vague light. Gradually, the light grew stronger, and soft voices surrounded him, though for a time he understood nothing of what was being said. When his eyes opened, he stared up at a brown ceiling.

"He's awake," a voice whispered, and suddenly Stacy's face appeared above his own.

"Stacy?"

"Yes, Jason."

"What happened? Where am I?"

"You're in the adobe," Stacy replied. "Do you remember what happened?"

Jason again saw Blount making off with Jenny. "Jenny? Is . . . is she all right?" he asked, making an effort to rise.

"Lie back down," Stacy said, forcing Jason back. "Somebody swiped your skull with a bullet, but you're going to be all right."

"Jenny?" Jason asked again.

"Jason, she . . ."

"Tell 'im," Jason heard Mel say. "He won't rest a second till you do."

"But he certainly won't rest then," Stacy replied.

"Blount has her, Jason," Mel said. "You told us that much over and over. So we don't know how she is. But Blount knows better than to hurt that girl. He'd have the whole territory after him."

Jason swung his feet to the floor. "How bad am I hurt?"

"I told you. A bruised skull," Stacy said. "You were knocked out. You've been out since yesterday afternoon."

"Help me stand."

"You sure?" Mel asked.

Stacy helped him sit on the edge of the bed. For a moment, the room swirled about him and then gradually settled into place. "What happened after I was shot?" he asked.

Mel picked up the story. "They stopped shooting when you went down and started to back off. When they were gone, Stacy and I rushed up to where you lay and brought you to the house. That was yesterday."

"I'm going to try and stand," Jason said, and he pushed himself to his feet. There was no dizziness, and after a moment he took a few steps around the room. "I can ride now," he told his friends.

"I ain't sure that's wise," Mel said.

"Will one of you saddle the sorrel and the other one get me something to eat? I've got no time to waste."

"I made some soup this morning," Mel said. "I'll get you a bowl."

"I'll eat it at the table," Jason said, and followed Mel to the kitchen.

"I'll saddle the sorrel," Stacy called after them.

Jason sat at the table. Mel brought a bowl of soup and set it before him, and returned for a cup of coffee. Jason spooned some of the soup into his mouth, chewing down on a nice chunk of beef.

"I never tasted anything better," he told Mel, helping himself to more.

"Then you must be sick," Mel said and laughed. "You never liked my soup before."

"The horses are ready," Stacy said, entering the kitchen.

"Horses?" Jason asked.

"We're riding with you," both men said together.

"And I'll need you both," Jason said to their surprise. "While I finish this soup, you boys pack us some food. No telling when we'll be back here, so make it a full sack. How much ammunition do we have?"

"Plenty," Stacy said. "You brought home enough to fight a war the last time you were in town."

"Pack it all," Jason told them.

Before Jason went outside, he stripped the bandage from his head and took a look at himself in the mirror. He was still pale, and there were shadows beneath his eyes. The bullet wound, already scabbing over, was just above his ear. The shot had come within a fraction of an inch to being fatal.

He found the holstered Peacemaker, checked its load, made sure the bullet belt was full, and buckled the gun on. The boys were saddled and waiting when he came outside. Mel had bags of supplies tied on behind their saddles. Jason walked to the sorrel, lifted the Winchester from its boot, and checked its load.

"You need any help getting up?" Mel asked.

Jason answered by putting his foot in the stirrup and swinging up.

"Guess you're all right," Mel said.

"Where're we going to start looking?" Stacy asked, as he and Mel fell in beside the sorrel.

"We'll start with the Taylor place. If Jenny isn't there, maybe we can get a line on where she is."

Stacy glanced at the sun. "Be dark when we get there if we don't hurry," he said.

"We'll need the darkness to get close," Jason replied. "If Blount's there, he and his men will start shooting the minute they see us."

His eyes strayed northwest to the Sierrita Mountains. A few threatening clouds floated over their bare craggy tops, their shadows turning the slopes a dark blue. As they rode, the wind touched down, rattling the dry brush and swirling up small dust eddies. After a few more miles, Jason pulled up.

"We'll wait here for darkness," he said, stepping down.

Mel and Stacy followed suit, each loosening the cinch of their mounts. While the horses nibbled at some nearby grass, the three men sought shade beneath an oak, their faces grim, their thoughts intent on the mission before them.

Jason's fear for Jenny was almost tangible. He was sure she had begun to think of him as a man she could respect, if nothing else. He had known a few women before, but never well. He did know that what he felt for Jenny was something new for him, an emotion so strong, he knew he'd never be rid of it, didn't want to be rid of it, wanted only to have her by his side always. He could think of only one thing: He had to get her back before Blount harmed her.

The more he thought about the succession of events, the more he knew that one of Blount's men had been watching the ranch full-time. Blount had known where Jenny lay in hiding, and the whole raid had been staged to draw Jason and his men into a fight to defend the valley, while Blount came in from behind and took Jenny. Jason felt like a fool, knowing Blount had been a step ahead of him.

But what were Blount's plans for Jenny? Did he intend to use her as a tool to force her to give up the ranch? Or could he have something more sinister in mind? Blount was an evil man of powerful emotions. He was also a strong man who acted on those emotions.

"Time to go," Jason said when the sun touched the western horizon. Walking to the sorrel, he tightened the cinch and swung into the saddle. The sun turned pinkish as they rode, then a bloody red as it sank out of sight. Giving the sorrel a soft knee, Jason urged the big horse into a canter.

They pulled up on the rise overlooking the headquarters of the Taylor spread. An ominous silence hung over everything, and only one tiny light winked up at them. Otherwise, the place lay in total darkness.

"That light is coming from the house," Mel whispered.

"Let's get down there," Jason said. "Don't do any shooting if you don't have to until we know if Jenny is in there. Then, if you have to, shoot. Shoot to kill."

Leaving their mounts tied to a bush, they made their way silently down the hillside.

By now, the darkness was intense, but Jason knew his way around the place pretty well. Soon, the outline of the house loomed up, and he touched the wall with an outstretched hand. Feeling his way along, he came to the window from which the dim light came. Peering inside, he saw nothing.

With Stacy and Mel following, Jason circled the house and came to the front door. Twisting the knob, he pushed the door in. Total darkness and silence. He took a step inside and paused to listen. Still he heard nothing.

Taking a match from his pocket, he scraped its head

against the door. For a dangerous moment, he was blinded by the sudden light. Then, outlines of furniture emerged, and he could see the room was empty.

He spotted a lantern on the mantel of the big fireplace and, crossing the room, lifted the glass and stuck the match to the wick. "The two of you stay here," he told Stacy and Mel. Then, lamp in hand, he began the search, entering each room carefully. After the final room, he gave up and returned to the parlor, only to find that Mel and Stacy were gone. Returning the lantern to the mantel, he left it burning and stepped outside.

The night had brightened considerably from a risen three-quarter moon. A mockingbird sang from a nearby tree, the song a taunt in Jason's ears. Hearing a scuffling from beside the house, Jason drew the Peacemaker and moved softly in that direction. Suddenly, Mel and Stacy came around the corner with a prisoner in tow.

"He was the only chicken in the henhouse," Mel said, giving the prisoner a shove. "But he's got an interesting story to tell."

"Bring him inside," Jason directed.

The man wore a bloody rag around his head. Obviously, he'd taken a shot during the gunfight back at the ranch.

"Now, tell him what you told us," Mel ordered, jamming the barrel of his six-gun into the man's side.

The man grunted with pain. "Some of the men didn't like it when Ben took the woman and run off," he said. "Ben never said anything about that being part of the plan. He was supposed to get in them rocks and open up on the bunch of you from up there. Most of the men packed their belongings, saddled up, and left when they got back. I was going myself when I felt a little better."

"Did Blount come back here?" Jason asked.

"Yeah, he circled back and picked up Sky Smith and Bones Skeleton. I saw him take some money from that little safe in his room."

"Did he have Jenny Taylor with him?"

"No. I reckon he stashed her someplace and then he came here."

"How long ago was this?"

"Several hours."

"What's your name?" Jason asked.

"Abe Carney."

"Why didn't you leave when the others did?" Jason continued.

"I took a bullet as you can see when we attacked your place. I'm feeling better and was about to ride out when you fellas sneaked up. But I ain't had nothing to do with what happened to that girl, and I ain't got no beef with you, Ward."

"Well, Abe, you're going to get off lucky," Jason said. "You fork a horse and ride out of here. Leave the country, and stay gone. If I see you around again, I'll swear out a warrant for you for murder, if I don't just shoot you instead."

Carney didn't seem to believe what he had heard. "You mean I can go?" he asked.

"You got ten minutes. You go with him, Mel. See that he forks a horse and rides out."

Abe Carney appeared at once to feel much better.

"Never saw a man so willing to ride," Mel said when he returned.

"What do we do now?" asked Stacy. "We can't follow Blount in the dark."

"No, we'll have to wait for daylight," Jason said, "but even then we'll need a tracker. Blount will cover his tracks. Anybody know one?"

Stacy and Mel looked at each other. "What about old Julio?" Stacy asked Mel.

"He ain't got no love for Ben Blount," Mel replied.

"Who is Julio?" Jason asked.

"Julio Sanchez," Mel said. "Stacy and I met him in New Castle one night. He'd lost his money in a poker game, and Stacy bought him a drink."

"He reminded me of someone I knew back in Yuma," Stacy said. "You remember Rick Cruz, the old man who worked in the woodshop? Julio looks a lot like Cruz. They're about the same age, and both are really bad poker players."

"We got to talking," Mel said, "and Stacy and I told him about your trouble with Blount. Seems Julio had a cabin up in the hills and was trapping for muskrats along a stream that crossed the Taylor spread. Blount came along. He and some of his men beat the old man up pretty bad. Then they went up to Julio's cabin, took his furs, and burned his cabin. Julio hates Blount's guts."

"But can he track?" Jason asked.

"Folks say that old man can track wind over rock," replied Mel.

"You go for the old man, Mel," Jason said. "Tell 'im I'll pay him for his time. Stacy and I will pick up Blount's trail come daylight. You and the old man can catch up."

"Chances are the offer of pay will insult him, but I'll tell 'im," Mel said. "But maybe we can get back here by sunup."

"Then shake a leg," Jason said. "Stacy and I will stay out of sight here and hope Blount returns."

"You reckon Blount intends to pick up more men somewhere along the way?" Stacy asked.

"If he's got money, he can hire all the men he needs,"

replied Jason. "The question is, how much money did he have?"

"Some talk in town about him selling off a lot of the cattle recently," Stacy said.

Chapter Twenty-one

Mel and Julio Sanchez rode in a little before sunup, a short time before Jason and Stacy were ready to start the search for Blount's trail. Jason had just finished cooking up potatoes, bacon, and coffee for breakfast.

"Jason, this is Julio Sanchez," Mel offered. "Julio, Jason Ward."

"Good to meet you, Julio," replied Jason. "Thanks for coming along on such short notice. Step down and join us. Might be a long time between hot meals from here on out."

"Don't mind if I do," Julio said, dismounting.

Jason gave him a fork, a plate, and a cup. "Help yourself to the food."

"Thanks," Julio said. "I told Mel here I wouldn't take any pay for this job. I have to settle a score with Blount myself."

Julio spoke English without an accent. And he did look a lot like Cruz, Jason decided. He had a slight paunch and, like Cruz, wore a full graying beard that matched the graying hair beneath his Texas hat. He wore a Colt .45 six-gun strapped to his thigh and a bandolier of bullets across his chest. Still, despite the gun and the bandolier, there was a fatherly air about him.

When they finished eating, Jason roped a solid-looking brown mare from the ET corral. In the barn, he found an *aparejos,* two large canvas pouches joined together so they could be thrown over a horse's back. Tough rawhide strings extended from the bottom of the pouches. When they were securely tied beneath the horse's belly, there was no danger the horse would lose the bags. Everyone lent a hand to gather the gear and stow it in the *aparejos,* and Jason tied it on the mare.

Julio had ridden in on a red mule with black markings, and Jason inquired if he'd like a fresh mount from the Taylor *remuda.* Julio declined, saying his mule—he called her Daze—though already ridden hard, was still fresh enough to ride any horse into the ground.

Ready at last, the four men rode out, with Julio in the lead. Circling the ranch house, Julio came upon a trail, swung from the saddle, and knelt to study the tracks.

"Should be five horses," Jason said, "if they took a pack animal."

"That's what these tracks say, and they were laid down about the right time," Julio replied, remounting.

"How can you tell about the time?" Jason asked.

"Check the hoof prints," Julio replied. "When they're real fresh, very little sand has run down into them. As they get older, more sand trickles in. I'd say these prints aren't much more than a day old."

The trail led south toward some low hills maybe forty or fifty miles away, and beyond those was the Mexican border. Jason hoped they'd catch up before then, but with the lead Blount had, maybe not. Still, he vowed to himself to chase the man all the way to South America if he had to.

The early morning air was cool and invigorating. Even

the desert was pleasant at that time of day. As usual, when the sun rose higher, it began to sap moisture from the grasses and plants, and even the low-growing shrubs and stunted trees began to look wilted. Only the cactus seemed to welcome the heat.

"Anybody need to stop for food?" Jason asked as noon approached. No one spoke. Jason had stowed some jerky in his saddlebag, and he passed that around for everyone to chew on.

A couple of hours later, Julio pulled up. "Some smoke up ahead," he said, indicating a spiraling column that rose fifty or a hundred feet into the air before the wind swept it away.

"How far ahead?" Jason asked.

"Maybe five miles," Julio replied.

"Could be them," Mel said. "What do you think, Julio?"

"They been riding awfully hard to suddenly pull up and stop," Julio said.

"Get us in as close as you can," Jason suggested to Julio, "and we'll have a look."

Julio led out, and the rest fell into line.

"Two more riders joined them here," Julio said, pulling up and indicating the merging sign.

"Wonder who it could be?" Mel asked.

"Reckon we'll find out when we catch up to them," Stacy replied.

As they approached the smoke, Julio became more careful, keeping to low ground when possible and staying on the brown, dried grass or rocks to keep their dust to a minimum.

"We should be able to see from up there," he said, pulling up behind a rise topped off with several jagged boulders protruding from the ridge like huge, uneven teeth.

"You stay here while Julio and I have a look," Jason said

to Mel and Stacy. Sliding from the saddle, he gave Stacy the sorrel's reins.

Julio led the way over some loose shale at the bottom of the rise and began to climb, Jason a step behind. Both had taken their rifles from their saddle boots and now carried the weapons in front them, making the climb on hands and knees more awkward. Jason, with eyes on the shale to keep from dislodging a slide, strayed a little to the right of the route chosen by Julio.

They reached the top and peered down at a small adobe hut with a thatched roof. The smoke, which had drawn them, came from the chimney and was little more than a few wisps now.

"You reckon they're inside?" Jason asked, whispering.

"I doubt it," Julio said. "I know the place. A fellow by the name of Troy Brooks lives here. He came into this country from Texas to do some prospecting. Rumor is he found some color. He rides into New Castle from time to time for supplies. Pays in dust."

"Maybe Blount and his boys knew about that dust," Jason said. "Maybe Blount felt he needed a bigger bankroll. If they've been here, I wouldn't bet two bits that Brooks is alive."

"Yeah, he's probably dead," Julio agreed.

The adobe sat in a ravine maybe a hundred-and-fifty feet wide, and Jason could see doors at front and back. There was also a small window facing them, and Jason decided there was probably a window on the off side as well. That being the case, he saw no way to reach the cabin under cover. He lay a moment trying to solve the problem of getting down there and in close before he was discovered, but nothing came to him. Either he would have to ride over to the cabin in clear view, or they'd have to wait till dark.

If they waited until dark, they would lose the rest of the day and night if Blount and his men weren't inside. He thought of Jenny and knew he had no choice.

"I'm going back down," he said to Julio. "I'll send Stacy and Mel up here. Then I'm going to circle east, cross over the ridge, and come up on the front of the cabin."

"You'll be taking an awful chance if they're holed up down there," Julio warned.

"I know, but I don't see any other way. We can't take the chance of waiting around till dark to find they're not here. The three of you be ready. If I draw fire, put as many bullets into that little window as you can. That ought to keep them from giving me their full attention."

"Reckon I'll ride with you," Mel said when Jason reached the bottom of the shale and explained his plan.

"I appreciate that, Mel," Jason said, "but you'll do me more good up there with Stacy and Julio. You can promise me one thing, though."

"What's that?"

"If something happens to me, get Jenny away from that thug."

"You can depend on it," Stacy and Mel replied together.

Jason watched as the two began their careful climb to join Julio, then he swung aboard the sorrel and, riding east, came to a cut in the ridge that allowed him to ride through. Before entering, he looked back. Stacy and Mel lay on either side of Julio at the crest of the ridge. Their eyes were on the hut below, and their rifles were ready.

The hut was no more than seventy-five yards from where Jason entered the ravine. As he rode in, he found he was facing the sun, which put him at a disadvantage. Pulling his hat low to shade his eyes, he rode forward, expecting any moment to see the door flung open and filled with exploding guns. The sorrel sensed his feelings and flung his head about nervously. "Easy, boy," Jason murmured. He placed a hand on the horse's neck to reassure him.

When Jason was twenty feet from the door, he pulled up. He slid from the saddle, walked to the door, and listened a moment. Nothing.

Drawing the Peacemaker, he gave the doorknob a twist and pushed. When he stepped inside, the heat was a blast in his face.

A man sat in a large chair, his profile to Jason as he stared toward a window. He was perfectly still and seemed totally unaware that Jason had entered the room. Jason might have thought him sleeping, but he could see the man's eyes. He was a big man, all bone and muscle. He wore no hat, and his thick, gray hair was swept straight back.

"Sir?" Jason asked, the Peacemaker aimed at the man just in case.

There was no answer, and Jason moved closer. He stopped in front of the rocker, and a chill shot through him. The right, lower portion of the man's face had been torn away by a bullet. His eyes still mirrored the pain and terror of his last moments. Obviously, the man had been shot at close range.

The room had been ransacked. Chairs were overturned, mattresses in the bunk beds had been slashed and their shucks scattered about the floor. Only the stove from which the smoke had come was intact.

Walking outside, Jason waved to his companions on the ridge. While he waited, he circled the house. Contrary to what he had thought, there was no window on that side. Instead, he found a lean-to in which maybe two horses had been recently stabled. Obviously, Blount and his friends had taken them.

He was sure he had the picture now. Blount and his party had come up on the adobe. The old man had invited them in. Once inside, they had shot him. Julio had said Troy Brooks had found gold. Maybe he had refused to show Blount his cache. That would have been enough for either of the outlaws to kill him.

"What do you think, Julio?" Jason asked when the others had gone through the hut.

"They knew about his gold," Julio said. "From the looks of things, I expect they found it."

"Should we bury him or ride on?" Stacy asked.

"Won't take long," Mel said.

"There's a shovel in the lean-to outside," Jason told them. "I'll get it and dig a grave. Julio, you get him ready for burial. There's a spring across the way. Stacy, you and Mel water our horses and top off our canteens. Feed the horses if there's grain in the lean-to."

As Jason dug a hole for Brooks, his mind was on Jenny. What chance had she to remain unharmed in the hands of scoundrels who would kill an old man who had done them no harm?

Before leaving, they gathered at the spring for a drink. When everyone had drunk their fill, the little pool still retained enough water for a second round for the horses.

Julio studied the sun a moment and turned to Jason. "I'm thinking we should spend the night here," he said. "Not much more than an hour of daylight left, and the horses can use the rest. Brooks kept plenty of oats on hand, enough for the horses to have a couple good feeds."

"Might as well put them in the lean-to then," Jason replied.

While the others saw to the horses, Jason set about cooking some supper. He made coffee, fried bacon, and cooked a pan of biscuits, baking enough for supper and breakfast, he hoped. Before they were finished eating, the sun went down in a burst of pink and red in the west.

"Is there a town nearby?" Jason asked as they sat around the fire.

"There's Naco," Julio said. "Why do you ask?"

"How big is Naco? How many saloons?"

"It's a little place on the border about twenty miles southwest of here," Julio said. "The people are mostly Mexican. When I was in there last, there were two cantinas."

"I expect we'll find them heading in that direction when we pick up the trail come morning," Jason said. "Blount has been riding a long time. He'll be thinking he's lost us, and he'll head for this Naco, knowing that even if we show up, all he has to do is slip across the border and lose us again."

Soon after that they spread their bedrolls several yards from the spring and bedded down. Silence came to the ravine, except for the snapping of a coal now and then as the fire burned down. A frog croaked from nearby, and beyond the ravine a coyote barked shrilly. There was also the rustle of small animals coming to the spring for water.

Something woke Jason, and he sat up and looked around. There was total silence now, and there was something menacing in the absence of any sound. Throwing his blanket aside, he started to rise when Julio reached out and held him.

"Wake the others," Julio whispered. "Sounds like we have visitors. I'm going out for a scout."

Julio was gone before Jason could ask him how he knew someone was near. But, following instructions, he crawled to where Mel and Stacy lay. Placing a hand softly over their mouths, he gently shook them awake.

"What the hell . . ." Mel said before Jason could stop him.

"Julio either saw or heard something," Jason told them. "He's out there now looking around."

"He say what it was?"

"No, but get your guns ready."

Crawling back to his own bedroll, Jason buckled the Peacemaker on and found the Winchester. Then he shook his boots out and slipped them on.

"The two of you stay here," he said. "I'm going to see about the horses." As quietly as he could, he crawled toward the hut and the lean-to. Then, suddenly outlined against the stars, he saw two men heading toward the lean-to.

"They'll be surprised as hell when they wake up in the morning and find their hosses gone," Jason heard one whisper. "Good idea the big man had sending us back to steal their mounts."

That's all Jason needed to hear. Bringing the Winchester to his shoulder, he squeezed off a shot at the nearest one. The explosion resounded through the ravine, and the man was knocked against the poles of the stalls. His grunt as he folded was sufficiently loud to be heard above the echoes that rumbled back and forth. Then the momentary silence was broken by the beat of shoe leather on dirt as the second man fled into the darkness. A moment later, Jason heard the sound of a running horse.

"Did you get one?" Mel asked from behind Jason.

"He's lying up there in front the lean-to," Jason told him.

They lay where they were for a second, then, rising, went to the fallen man. A moment later, Julio appeared, identifying himself before he came in. He knelt beside the man, struck a match, and held it before the man's face. Jason recognized the face of Abe Carney, the man he had told to leave the country.

"He didn't take your advice," Stacy said. "Must have known where Blount was headed and caught up with him."

"You got him in the chest, but he ain't dead yet," Julio told them.

"Let's get him back to the fire, Julio," Jason said. "Maybe he can tell us what shape Jenny is in."

"If he lives long enough," Julio replied.

Mel and Jason took an arm each, and Julio and Stacy took Carney's legs. Together they carried him to their camp.

"We need more light," Jason said and piled more wood on the fire.

Mel's prognosis of a quick death for Carney seemed about right. His face was pasty white and his eyes were surprisingly filled with tears, reflecting the pain he was feeling.

"If you don't do something, I'm gonna die," he managed to whisper.

"First, you tell me about Jenny Taylor," Jason said. "Has she been harmed in any way?"

"She's . . . Blount's got her," Carney whispered.

"We know that, but how is she?"

"Ben won't let any of the rest get near her. He's keeping her for his self."

"Has he harmed her in any way?" Jason asked.

"He ain't done nothing yet," Carney said.

Then Abe Carney died, his eyelids closing halfway.

"He was willing to talk," Julio said. "Wish he could have lived a little longer. Maybe he could have told us exactly where they were going. But I guess we know that anyway."

Jason felt nothing but frustration. They'd now been away

from the ranch for a week, and they were no nearer rescuing Jenny than they'd been the very first day.

"There's no telling how long before we'll catch up to Blount," he told Mel and Stacy. "I want the two of you to return to the ranch. Julio and I will stay on Blount's trail. I'll see you when we catch up to him and free Jenny. Meanwhile, keep the ranch up."

The order met with protests, but Jason had his way.

Julio and Jason watched Mel and Stacy ride north the next morning. Then they circled the ravine to pick up the trail they'd been following for days now. "They rode southeast," Julio said.

"Naco?" Jason asked.

"If you keep on in the same direction."

"Well, let's get after them, Julio."

Chapter Twenty-two

They rode hard, talking little. The morning waned and, as midday approached, the sun beat down fiercely. Near sundown, Julio led the way into a small canyon that ran into the heart of mountains whose foothills they had been skirting most of the day.

A small spring of cold mountain water ran from beneath some rocks. "Reckon we should spend the night here," Julio said, pulling up before the spring. "You tend the horses, and I'll cook us up some food."

"You tired of my cooking, Julio?" Jason asked and chuckled.

"It's your biscuits, son," Julio said. "I'm going to show you how biscuits should be cooked."

"I'll admit yours are better, Julio," Jason said later as they were eating. "They beat mine by a mile."

When they made Naco a little after sunup the next morning, both riders and horses were spent from the hard ride. But the thought that Jenny might be there gave Jason fresh energy.

"You're looking beat," Julio observed. "Want to hole up for awhile, maybe get a meal before we mosey around and see if they're here?"

"I couldn't rest," Jason said. "I'd be thinking of Jenny all the while. What if they decided to leave while we're resting? Let's look for them now. You know anybody here?"

"I know the liveryman."

"We might get a lead from him. Where is the livery?" Jason asked.

"Right there," Julio replied and pointed to a large barn and corral a block down the street. "His name is Burly Saxton."

"Let's go see Mr. Saxton."

Jason rode behind Julio a little nervously. He had the feeling that unfriendly eyes were on them. A moment later, they pulled up before the livery and swung down.

Burly Saxton made no appearance, and the two walked beneath the long, high aisle of the barn. The smell of fresh horse dung was strong, but no man who depended on horses found the smell unpleasant. Julio stepped to the tack room and pounded on the closed door. A moment later, a large disheveled man pushed the door open and looked out.

"What you want?" he asked, rubbing sleep from his eyes.

"Julio Sanchez, Burly."

Burly Saxton took his fists from his eyes and gave Julio a quick look. "Why Julio, you old son of a gun! How are you?"

"I'm fine, Burly. This here is Jason Ward. We need some information."

"Yeah, *amigo*."

Saxton, Jason decided, was called Burly because of his size. He was a powerful-looking man with lots of brown hair and a thick mustache to match.

"We're chasing three men, maybe four. We think they may be in town, Mr. Saxton," Jason said. "They took a woman captive up at New Castle. Have you seen anyone like that?"

"Seen two men with five horses," Saxton said. "They come by here about midnight and left their mounts. Didn't see no woman, though."

"Are the horses still here?" Julio asked.

"Right back there."

"Can we see them?"

"Don't see why not. You say they took a woman? Why if I'd knowed that I'd have knocked their heads together last night instead of taking in their horses. Anything I can do to help out, Julio?"

"We'll take care of them, Burly, if we find them here," Julio replied.

Julio led the way back to the stalls and checked the brands on the horses. "Two have ET brands," he said. "I don't know the others."

"That's Blount's big gray," Jason agreed. "I'd know him anywhere."

"We'll have some breakfast and ask a few questions," Julio said, as they made their way back along the board-walk before still unopened stores.

"You got a special place in mind?" Jason asked.

"Just ahead here." Julio pointed to a sign that read *Hargrove's Breakfast, Lunch, and Dinner*. "Dan Hargrove and I did some prospecting together some years back."

"Anybody in Arizona you don't know?" Jason asked.

"I been around a long time, son," Julio said. "Guess I got to know a few folks."

The cafe was empty when they entered and, glancing at a clock on a wall, Jason knew why. The clock read 5:30, too early for most folks to be up. They sat at a counter up front and soon a short robust man wearing a stained apron appeared to take their orders.

"I don't believe it!" he said, smiling broadly when he saw Julio. "When did you hit town, Julio?"

"Know it's early, Dan, but how about some breakfast for me and my friend?"

"I can give you a slice of ham and some eggs, and I just took the first loaf of bread out of my oven," Dan Hargrove said.

"Add some coffee to that, and we'll be happy." Julio gestured toward Jason. "Like you to meet a friend of mine, Dan. This is Jason Ward."

Jason and Hargrove shook. "Any friend of Julio's, Mr. Ward," and with that, Hargrove returned to his kitchen.

"I can smell that bread out here," Jason said.

"Making my stomach beg," replied Julio.

In what seemed like a very short time, Hargrove returned with a plate in each hand and set them before Jason and Julio. The slices of ham were as thick as steaks, and the piles of scrambled eggs looked overly generous as well. Slices of buttered bread covered the rest of the plates.

Setting cups of coffee before them, Hargrove poured a cup for himself, pulled out a stool and settled his hefty bottom on it, facing them across the counter. "Now tell me what brings you to Naco, Julio," he said.

"We're looking for some men, Dan," Julio said. "They're mean as rattlers and they took a woman up at New Castle. We know they're here; we seen their horses in Burly's livery."

Jason gave a quick description of Blount, Smith, and Skeleton. "Wonder if you've seen anything of them?"

"When do you think they come into town?" Hargrove asked.

"About midnight."

"I was closed then, and nobody like that has been in so far this morning. Reckon I can't help you. Bet they're staying at the hotel."

"Which hotel?" Jason asked.

"The Alhambra. Just across the street."

"Fancy name for something that looks as seedy as that," Julio said, glancing out the window at the hotel.

They finished their meal hurriedly and were halfway across the street when Bones Skeleton came out of the Alhambra. He saw Jason and Julio, froze for a moment, and then turned back.

"Just a minute there, Skeleton!" Jason yelled, and went for the Peacemaker.

Skeleton whirled to face them, drawing his own gun. The two guns went off at about the same moment. Skeleton's bullet sent Jason's hat sailing off his head, while Jason's bullet smashed into the glass door of the hotel. Skeleton fell behind the hitch-rail post and continued firing.

Both Jason and Julio hit the dried mud of the street as Skeleton's bullets kicked up dust around them. Jason's next bullet hit the post behind which Skeleton lay. Then, Julio's rifle exploded, blowing away half the post and hitting Skeleton, who tried to push himself up and, failing, sank down again.

"I think I got 'im, Jason!" Julio said.

"We best be sure, Julio," Jason warned.

Guns drawn, they walked to where Skeleton lay. "Your rifle took him out, Julio," Jason said. Now let's get inside and get the others."

Scrambling up, they made a run for the hotel. Before they made it inside, a second gun opened up on them from the broken window of the hotel.

"Let's split up!" Jason yelled and angled right as he ran.

Julio ran for the other side of the hotel. The shooter ignored Julio and kept firing at Jason. A bullet fanned Jason's cheek, and another caught the sleeve of his shirt. Only when Jason made the corner of the hotel and was out of sight did the shooting stop.

Julio rounded the corner opposite Jason, and the two began easing along the front of the hotel, closely hugging the wall, as Jason fired a couple of bullets into the window through which the shots had come. He reached the window and, crouching low, eased his head up and peered inside.

"Don't see him!" he whispered to Julio. Both men rushed through the door of the hotel and hit the floor as a gun opened up from behind a settee, spraying bullets into the doorway where the two had been.

Both Julio and Jason fired into the flimsy couch. Jason heard a gasp as something hit the floor. "Keep me covered," he said to Julio.

Crawling to the end of the settee, Jason peered around it. Sky Smith was sprawled on his back. He heaved a sigh as Jason watched, and then was still.

"It's Smith, and he's dead," he told Julio.

After a moment, a bald head peered over the hotel desk and looked anxiously around.

Jason crossed to the desk. "Let me have a look at your register, mister."

"I can't do that," the clerk said.

Jason reached for the register and turned it around, running his finger down the list of names and room numbers. "They're in room twenty upstairs," he told Julio.

Jason hit the stairs with Julio hot on his heels. Slowing down when they reached the second floor, they moved cautiously along the hallway in search of room twenty. Finding the room, each took a side, and Jason gave the knob a twist.

Expecting a hail of bullets, he shoved the door in and sprawled to the floor inside. Nothing happened, and he cautiously pushed himself up and looked around.

The room was empty except for Jenny. She lay motionless on the bed, hands and feet bound, a gag in her mouth. From all appearances, she was either asleep or dead.

Jason removed the gag and began to untie the rope that bound her hands while Julio worked at the one around her ankles. There was still no sign of life when Jenny was free. Jason put a finger to her neck to check her pulse. "She's alive," he said to Julio. "Go downstairs and tell that clerk to give you a little liquor. A good sip might revive her."

"Be right back," Julio said and hustled out.

While Julio was gone, Jason paced the room, fearful of Jenny's condition. What had they done to her? Her color was all washed out and she looked as though she hadn't had food for several days.

Julio returned with a glass of what looked like water. "Tequila," he said in answer to Jason's look. Going to the bed, he lifted Jenny's head and held the glass to her lips, forcing some of the fiery liquid into her mouth. She shuddered as the tequila went down. Then she opened her eyes and looked up into Julio's face and then at Jason, who stood next to Julio.

"You came," she murmured softly. "I knew you were back there somewhere."

"We got Skeleton outside," Jason said. "Who was up here with you?"

"Blount," she said, "he went out the window."

Julio went to the window and looked down. "A fire escape," he said.

Jason sat on the bed and took her hands. "Thank God you're all right," he said.

"Help me up," Jenny replied.

He helped her from the bed. Jenny stood a little shakily and, a moment later, took a few steps about the room. "Let's get out of this filthy place," she said. Taking her arm, Jason led her from the room and down the stairs with Julio following.

The shooting had drawn a crowd, including a tall sour-looking man with a badge.

"Reckon you better tell me what's going on here," he said, his hand on the handle of a Colt .45.

Dan Hargrove pushed through the crowd. "I know these folks, Sheriff," he said. "They been chasing some galoots who'd kidnapped this woman."

The sheriff relaxed a little. "Tell me about it," he said, leading the three of them to a long wooden bench and indicating they were to sit.

Julio spent a few minutes relating the high points of what had happened over the past several days, while Jason was content to sit beside Jenny, his arm self-consciously around her slim waist.

"That's quite a story," the sheriff said when Julio was finished. "But I reckon you've lost them that got away. They'll be in Mexico by now if they've got any sense. Reckon you folks will want to rest up a bit before you start home," he said. "Otto, you fix them up with some rooms and be sure they're treated right," he said to the clerk.

"Two rooms side-by-side with a connecting door," Jason said when they were inside about to sign the register. "But not room twenty."

"No, not room twenty," Jenny agreed.

"I got just what you want," the clerk replied. "Rooms twenty-three and twenty-four."

By then, the crowd had begun to drift away. Jason signed the register for all three and ordered a tub of hot water for each room. He was sweaty and dirty from the roll in the dusty street, and Jenny looked as if she would appreciate a bath as well.

When Jason looked around, Julio was gone. "Did you see him leave?" he asked Jenny.

"He just turned around and went out the front door," Jenny said.

"Did he say anything?"

"No."

"Who's going to pay for that broken window?" the clerk asked.

Jason tossed some money on the desk. "That should take care of the window and our rooms. If it doesn't, tell the sheriff to get some money from the man they just hauled off to the undertaker. I expect he'll have some on him. Maybe quite a lot."

Walking to the front door of the hotel, Jason stepped outside and looked both ways in search of Julio. He stood there several moments before deciding that Julio must have gone off to look up some of his friends. Then, returning to Jenny, he took her arm and led her toward the stairs. Once upstairs, they walked along the hallway and found their rooms.

"Don't open the door for anyone but Julio or me," he warned. Once they were inside Jenny's room, he led her to the bed. When she sat, he leaned down and removed her shoes.

The tubs of hot water arrived. "Must have had the water already heated," Jason said. Then, walking to the connecting door, he exited into his and Julio's room. "I'll leave the door cracked a little," he called back to Jenny. "Yell if you want anything."

He tested the water and found it comfortably warm. Then, conscious of the slightly cracked connecting door, he stripped down and stepped into the tub. From the other room, he heard Jenny's splashes and was embarrassed at the vision they called forth in his mind.

He couldn't stretch his legs out in the tub, but he sank as low in the water as he could. He tried to remember the last time he had soaked in a hot tub. Closing his eyes, he felt his weary muscles begin to lose some of their aches.

He had dusted off his clothes and was dressed when Jenny knocked. "Are you dressed?" she asked.

"Come in," he called.

She had never looked more beautiful. She had washed her hair and brushed it back and managed to get most of the dust and grit from her clothes. Despite their still-soiled condition, she looked every bit the refined lady.

"I need to buy some things," she said. "I saw a mercantile shop down the street. Do you think we might go there before we get something to eat?"

"Sure thing," Jason replied, and taking her arm, escorted her down the stairs, into the street, and along the boardwalk till they reached the store.

There Jenny bought a white shirt that could have been worn by a man but for the embroidered flowers on the pocket. She also bought a brown riding skirt with a split in the rear, and a pair of half boots.

"I hope you've got some money," she said to Jason when they reached the cash register.

"I have," he said and counted out the figure the clerk said Jenny owed.

They found Julio in the cafe across the street from the hotel busy with a bowl of beef stew.

"Where have you been?" Jason asked. "I was a little worried when you left without saying anything."

"Recommend you try the stew," Julio said as they sat down. He ignored Jason's question.

Jason arranged Jenny's packages on the extra chair. "I'll have the stew," he said when Hargrove came to take their order. "How about you, Jenny?"

"The same."

"When are we heading out again after Blount?" Julio asked as they ate.

"I'm not," Jason said. "I'm taking Jenny back to the ranch."

Julio was silent for a long moment.

"What about you, Julio?" Jason asked. "You've done everything I asked of you and more. I won't insult you by offering you pay again, but I'd like you to come back with us."

"Reckon I'll poke around across the border a bit."

"I'm not sure I want to leave you down here alone," Jason said.

"Don't worry about me," Julio said. "I got some kinfolk across the border a little way. I ain't seen them in a long time. Thought I might look them up while I'm close."

"Will you let me know if you hear anything about Blount?" Jason asked.

"You can bet on it."

"And promise me something else."

"What's that?"

"If you come across Blount, don't try and tackle him alone."

Julio finished his stew and pushed back from the table. "Guess I'll be on my way," he said. Standing, he reached for his hat and headed for the street.

"He doesn't sound like he looks," Jenny said.

"How's that?"

"Well, he's Spanish or Mexican, but he speaks English as well as anyone I know. How long have you known him?" Jenny asked.

"No more than a few weeks."

"But you act as if you've known him longer. You like him, don't you?"

"I like him very much," Jason said. "He's a fine man."

Chapter Twenty-three

Much had to be done on the ranch before winter came. Stacy cut and stacked hay while Jason and Mel made a fall roundup to brand the new calves. Jason found something to do at night as well. Strapping the Peacemaker on after supper each night, he walked outside and practiced his draw. Later, he read from the books he had picked up in town, especially enjoying two by Charles Dickens: *Oliver Twist* and *David Copperfield*. Jason knew nothing of slums such as Dickens described, but he could appreciate the hardships faced by the characters.

"Maybe you should practice aiming that Peacemaker in daylight a little," Mel said, as he watched Jason practice one evening. "You should begin using real ammunition too."

Jason took Mel's advice and practiced both drawing and shooting for the next few days. His aim, always good, improved along with his speed.

Rusty had always cautioned Jason that a fast draw meant little if you didn't hit what you aimed at. Though he practiced for a speedy draw, his main concern was a smooth action and a steady hand as he brought the Peacemaker into position and squeezed the trigger.

Regardless of the hard work, Jenny was never far from Jason's mind. Nor could he settle into the routine life of a rancher after returning from Naco with Jenny. He couldn't believe Blount would simply disappear and give up title to a fortune in ranch land and cattle without an attempt to regain control. Jason was constantly alert when he worked the ranch or rode to and from New Castle. He warned Jenny, as well as Mel and Stacy, to be on guard as well.

The others didn't seem as convinced. "He won't dare return," Stacy claimed, "as long as you and Jenny are around to swear to his treachery. Marshal Gruber is after him as well."

The letter from Jenny's father, the paper signed by Tolbert, and Jenny's kidnapping had finally convinced Marshal Gruber that Ben Blount had murdered Evan Taylor, and Blount was now a posted outlaw with a price on his head.

Jason's feelings for Jenny also kept him in an anxious state. He was now certain he was in love with her, but he couldn't convince himself she cared for him. He had never been in love before, and he had no idea how to approach a woman without possibly offending her. The very thought of declaring himself to Jenny instantly produced sweaty palms and armpits.

To help Jenny with the cooking and work around the house, Jason hired a middle-aged Mexican woman named Estelle Montez. Asked how she had kept her figure, she replied, "Hard work."

When she came to the ranch, she took charge of the kitchen and, with Jenny's help, turned out food that kept the men looking forward to the next meal. She planted a garden for fresh vegetables, and talked Jason into buying fruit trees whose planting she oversaw. Her presence and the changes she made gave the ranch a feeling of permanency.

Then Julio Sanchez returned.

He rode in at sundown one evening and found everyone at the supper table. Calling for Estelle to bring another plate and slapping Julio on the back with affection, Jason found a chair for the Mexican. Jason also noted Julio's covert assessment of Estelle as she served him.

"Julio, meet Estelle Montez," he said, a smile hovering about his lips. "Estelle, this is the man you've heard us talk about so much."

Julio stood and astonished everyone by delivering a courtly bow and saying, "I'm honored, Señora."

"Señorita, sir," Estelle replied and curtsied.

He's a sly old fox, Jason thought to himself, and then thought how nice it would be if two such good people got together.

Julio's preoccupation with the ranch's new cook made him forget for a moment the news he had brought. "Did you hear anything of Blount south of the border?" Jason asked, reminding him.

"Nada," Julio said. "I looked around and put out the word, but got nothing in return. I don't think he's in that country."

"Now you men will take your coffee outside to the picnic table by the stream and discuss that business out there," Estelle announced. "Jenny and I will see to the kitchen."

"I guess I better stay and help," Julio said, as the others willingly filed out.

They found seats around the table, saying little, and listened to the murmuring of the stream.

"Where do you think he might be, Jason?" Mel finally asked.

"I have no idea," Jason replied.

Jenny came from the house and joined them. "I think Julio's crush on Estelle is building," she said and smiled. "He insisted I join the three of you out here."

"Make a good pair," Mel said.

Everyone happily agreed.

After breakfast the next morning, Jason packed enough supplies to last for several days and saddled the sorrel.

"Where you headed, boss?" Stacy asked, coming in from the barn.

"Thought I might look around some," Jason replied. "There's nothing you and Mel can't handle here, and I'll be back in a few days."

"Did you tell Miss Jenny you were going?"

"You can tell her if she asks," Jason replied and, climbing astride the sorrel, rode toward the distant line of hills.

"Where is he going?" asked Mel, who had joined Stacy.

"Said he was going to scout around."

"Ben Blount is still on his mind," Mel replied. "He isn't satisfied Blount won't return and make more trouble."

"I hope he's wrong, and we've heard the last of that man," Stacy said thoughtfully.

Jason's mind *was* on Ben Blount. Regardless of what the others thought, he couldn't believe Blount was a man who would give up his claim to the Taylor ranch so easily. Nor would Blount be content until he took his revenge on Jason. In fact, Jason's instincts told him that Blount was very likely lying out in the hills, waiting for an opportunity to strike.

By the time Jason made the foothills, the day was almost over. Still, he decided to begin his search. He worked methodically in and out of the ravines and valleys looking for signs of riders or campsites. As night came on, he sought a place to camp. Coming upon a coulee from which flowed a small stream, he turned in. About a fifty yards up the rift, he found the spring shaded by several willows and poplar.

Stripping the gear from the sorrel, he let the horse drink. After rubbing him down with a handful of grass, he staked him. As the sorrel grazed, Jason gathered wood, built a small fire, and cooked his supper. After eating, he let the fire die down, took his bedroll some distance from the coals, and bedded down, the Peacemaker and Winchester close at hand.

As he lay on his blanket and watched the coals of the fire gradually turn from red to gray, he thought of what he would do if he found Blount. He had to kill the man or spend the rest of his life looking over his shoulder.

A simple truth suddenly came clear to him. Ben Blount was an evil man, and the truly wicked do not reform. They go on and on wreaking their evil upon men until someone puts a stop to it. He knew then that his determination to rid the world of Blount did not merely spring from the wrongs the man had done him. He had to make sure that Blount never wronged anyone else.

Overhead, night birds twittered. The sound, ordinarily a pleasant one, contrasted strangely with Jason's present mood. A coyote yammered at the night, and somewhere a quail called plaintively. Turning on his side, he forced his mind free of all thoughts of Blount and, finally, slept.

Jason spent a week and a half working his way around the valley. He saw signs of an occasional rider who had taken a shortcut through the range and, from time to time, scared up ET cattle, even a few of his own, in the brush along the foothills, but he found nothing that resembled a permanent campsite. Finally, he gave up and decided to go home, hoping he had disproved his instincts that Blount had returned.

Chapter Twenty-four

When Jason rode into the valley again, he found the house strangely quiet. Hurriedly, he searched the rooms, fearful that something had happened in his absence, but everything seemed in place. In fact, a fire burned in the stove.

Hearing riders come into the yard, he drew the Peacemaker and went to the door. Mel and Stacy had dismounted and were standing beside the sorrel looking the horse over. Holstering the Peacemaker, Jason stepped through the door.

"Well, you're back!" Stacy said. "We thought those hills might have swallowed you!"

"What did you find out there?" Mel asked, following Jason and Stacy back inside the house.

"Nothing. Neither hide nor hair of Blount."

Mel and Jason found chairs around the table while Stacy poured three cups of hot coffee, brought them to the table, and found a chair for himself.

"Where's Jenny?" Jason asked.

"She's back at the Taylor ranch. She left the same day

165

you did. Took the letter her father wrote and the paper Tolbert signed, hired a lawyer, and got the phony will revoked. As Evan Taylor's sole survivor, the ranch now belongs to her. Hired herself a general overseer, as she calls him, and a foreman, who's in charge of the cattle."

"Where did she find a . . . what did you call him? An overseer?"

"That's right," replied Mel.

"His name is Tee Martin," Stacy joked. "A crusty old fellow who'll bite your head off if you mess with his boss."

"Got a good *segundo* too. Tee brought him in from a ranch near Phoenix. Name's Jack Crowe. Seems like a good man and knows cattle. He's already got the herd rounded up and made a count. Jenny owns a herd of more than three thousand cattle. That's small compared to what the count was a year or so ago, but it's a good start."

"Where's Estelle?" Jason asked.

Mel and Stacy laughed. "Julio up and asked her to marry him," Mel said. "They bought the old Gibson place north of here. They're cleaning that place up and plan to start themselves a herd."

Jason couldn't have been more pleased. "Reckon I shouldn't be surprised," he said. "I remember they were getting along real well when I left."

"They're a good pair, and we all owe them a lot," Stacy said.

"Well, we got work to do," Mel said, pushing back from the table.

"I'll lend a hand," Jason told him.

"No," Mel insisted. "You have to be tired from all that riding. You finish your coffee and get some rest."

When they were gone, Jason's thoughts turned to Jenny. She was now a wealthy woman and would be a power in the county. He'd had only the faintest hope before this that she might consider marrying him. Now he knew she was completely out of his reach. Still, he had to see her. He would rest up tonight and ride over to the Taylor place come morning.

The improvements in the grounds and on the buildings had already begun. The trash had been hauled away and the yards cleaned. The main house had a new coat of white paint, and the windows had been repaired.

Jason pulled the sorrel up at the hitch rail before the house. He swung down as Tee Martin came from inside. "Look who's come calling," he said, and chuckled. "The boss has been staring across the range in your direction for days."

"Why would she do that?" Jason asked, his neck turning red.

Tee laughed again. "You're telling me you don't know?" he asked.

"Well, where is she?" Jason replied hastily.

"She got tired of sitting around the house and went out for a ride," Tee replied. "She should be back soon."

"Mel and Stacy told me Jenny had hired you to oversee the place. How's everything coming along?"

"There's lots of work to do, but we've made a start. Beats getting shaken to death driving a stage," Tee added.

"I can see that," Jason said, admiring the confident look about the old man.

Jenny rode into the yard a few moments later. Pulling up at the corral, she swung down. A stable hand came for her mount. Jason, leading the sorrel, walked down to meet her, followed by Tee.

"When did you get back?" Jenny asked, greeting Jason

warmly. Still, he sensed a difference in her. She seemed older and more secure.

"Came in yesterday. Mel and Stacy told me the good news."

"I owe you so much, Jason. All this would never have happened without you. Tell me what I can do for you to help make it up."

"You owe me nothing. Seeing you on this place is pay enough."

"It's all your work," she said.

"You two must have a lot of talking to do," Tee said. "I'll take care of the horse, Jason." Turning to Jenny, he said, "Maybe you should take him inside. Bet he didn't have breakfast before he charged over here to see you."

Jason's face felt like it would bleed.

"He's wrong," Jenny teased once they were inside. "You did have breakfast, didn't you."

"Afraid not," Jason managed to say.

"Would you like some?" Jenny asked.

"No, but I could use a cup of coffee."

Jenny led him through the house to the dining room. "Sit there," she said, indicating the dining-room table. "I'll get us some coffee."

She soon returned with two steaming cups and sat across from Jason. She did seem different than when he'd last seen her. There was an ease about her, a confidence she had lacked before. Of course, she was now one of the biggest ranchers in the county.

"Well, I better be going," Jason said, rising. "I just wanted to see how you were doing."

They rose together, and Jenny followed him through the house to the front door. "Thanks again," she said, reaching for Jason's hand.

The palm of her hand felt warm and moist, and Jason suddenly felt like raising it to his lips. Then somehow his arm wound up around Jenny's slim waist. Her body against his and the faint scent of gardenias gave him a dizzy feeling.

He would never know how it happened, but suddenly her face was turned up to his and, lowering his lips to hers, he kissed her. The kiss wiped any thoughts other than her firm, warm body and soft lips from his mind, and Jason felt he knew what Heaven must be like.

Finally, he broke the kiss and stared down into Jenny's shining blue eyes. "I . . . I love you, Jenny," he managed to say. "I think I have from the first moment I saw you, but . . . I . . ."

Jenny raised her fingers to his lips. "I love you too, Jason. Nothing else matters. Isn't that true?"

Jason was so stunned he couldn't think for a moment. He had never imagined that someone like Jenny Taylor, a refined, educated woman, could love a simple cowboy, though he was now the owner of his own ranch. When he spoke, it was as if the sound came from another person inside him.

"Will you marry me, Jenny?"

"Of course I will, silly," Jenny replied and laughed. "If you hadn't asked me, I'd have proposed to you."

"We'll have to wait for one thing," Jason said.

"What?"

"Till Ben Blount is caught and jailed."

Tee met him halfway between barn and house and gave him the sorrel's reins. Sensing something different about Jason, he looked at Jenny who stood on the porch. There was something different about her as well. The situation didn't register with the old stage driver for a moment. Then he smiled broadly. *Darned if they didn't have an understanding*, he thought, and a broad smile rippled the wrinkles of his face.

Chapter Twenty-five

"Whoa, Denver," Jack Crowe said to the black he was riding. The horse pulled up, and Crowe swung down. Kneeling, he studied the tracks that led away toward the Sierrita Mountains to the northwest. Climbing aboard the horse again, he crisscrossed the trail a couple of times, estimating the count and studying the tracks of the riders that herded the cattle along. He made the count to be about fifty and the riders to be no more than five.

This was the fourth small herd cut out of the Taylor herds Crowe had come across in a week. Somebody was getting ready to make a run with a herd to the border. Turning the black around, he headed back to the ranch.

Crowe had known Tee Martin all his life and, at the age of twenty, he had ridden shotgun with Tee for a couple of years when the stage carried something that might invite a holdup. Bored by the long rides, he had drifted into cattle work and made a name for himself as a top hand. He had jumped at the chance of the *segundo's* job on the Taylor Ranch when Tee made the offer, and he didn't mean to stand by and see the ranch's cattle rustled.

At thirty, Jack Cowe was not a big man, but he possessed surprising strength in his wiry frame. Though not what women might call handsome, the features of his square face and jaw would not be considered homely. His brown hair was always well trimmed, and his gray eyes most often beamed with good humor.

"They cut out another fifty head," he called to Tee when he rode into the ranch-house yard.

Tee rose from the rocker. "Did they head for the Sierritas again?" he asked.

"In about the same direction," Jack said.

Jenny came from the house. Jack lifted his hat from his head. "Ma'am," he greeted Jenny.

"I heard," Jenny said to Tee. "It's time we put a stop to it. Tee, call in a few of the hands. We'll ride out and see what we can come up with."

"You gonna ride too, Jenny?" Tee asked.

"Why not? They're my cattle."

"How many riders pushing that herd, Jack?" Tee asked.

"I counted five different sets of tracks."

"Then round up a half-dozen riders," Tee ordered. "See that they're armed with rifles and six-guns. I'll bring along extra ammunitions. Saddle up a mount for Miss Jenny and me. We'll be ready to ride in ten minutes."

"Tell Cookie to pack some food!" Jenny called to Jack's departing back. Tell him we'll need enough for four or five days, just in case," she added.

Jack and six ET riders were waiting before the house when Jenny and Tee emerged. Jenny had changed into riding clothes and wore a holstered six-gun strapped about her waist. Both she and Tee carried Winchesters.

"Lead out, Jack," Tee said when they were mounted.

"Hope they don't see our dust," Tee said after they had ridden for a time.

"I expect they're too far away for that," Jack replied.

When they reached the spot where Jack had spotted the trail, the party pulled up. After studying the sign for a few moments, Tee turned to Jack. "I count about the same as you and, unless they turn off, they're headed straight for the Sierritas. Let's push on hard. If they stop for the night, we might come up to them."

But the rustlers didn't stop and, afraid of losing the trail, Tee called a halt shortly after dark and ordered some food cooked up.

Tim Golden, the youngest among the riders and a man used to doing the extra chores, went to the packhorse and returned with the food bag.

"You start a fire, Tim," Jenny said. "I'll do the cooking."

"Dig a hole so we can hide the fire," Tee said to another rider.

"We ain't got no shovel," the rider said.

"Then, by durn, use your hands!" Tee snapped.

When the hole was dug, Tim quickly started a small fire.

"You can boil some coffee now, Tim," Jenny said and, taking a cooked ham from the food bag, she began to slice off steaks.

Tim brought a water bag from the packhorse, filled the coffee pot, and set it near the fire to boil. When the water began to bubble, he poured in some grounds.

"Unsaddle the horses and stake them out," Jack told the four idle riders.

Meanwhile, Jenny had cut several potatoes into slices. Chopping up some of the ham for grease, she added chopped onion to the potatoes and put the mixture on to cook. She put the ham steaks into another pan and, raking a few coals from the fire, set the steaks on these to warm them up. Next, she took a loaf of bread from the food bag and sliced it. Soon the crew settled down to a meal of bread, fried potatoes, baked ham, and coffee.

"We'd better keep watch," Tee suggested to Jack when they had eaten and were preparing for bed.

"We'll stand two hours on," Jack said. "That way everyone gets a good amount of sleep. I'll stand the first and then wake Butch."

Late the next day they rode into the foothills of the Sierritas and, though they had gained, they were still well behind the hard-pushed herd. The trail wound through the low hills and sometimes over a low hogback.

On the second day, the trail turned off into a canyon. Soon the ground became damp and, presently, they came upon the remains of a small stream which settled into the dry ground and gave out.

The grass in the valley grew thick and abundant along the little stream. From time to time they saw places where the rustlers had let the herd settle in to graze. Soon, from a distance, they heard the bawling of cattle.

"Hold up!" Tee ordered.

In the silence, the lowing of the cattle became more distinct.

"How far would you say, Jack," Tee asked.

"A quarter mile, no more."

"Let's water the horses," Tee said, "and then we'll ride into them willows over there. Jenny, you and the boys will stay there while Jack and I scout ahead. If we don't return in thirty minutes, the rest of you ride for help." He looked at Jenny and continued. "Under no circumstances will you ride in there looking for us."

Jenny remained silent.

Jack and Tee topped of their canteens, mounted, and, leaving the others behind, took to the brush.

When they neared the cattle, they caught the smell of burnt hide. "They're branding," Jack said.

Tee signaled a stop. "Let's get down here and move in on foot."

Snaking their way through the brush, they came to where the grass had been thoroughly grazed. From there, they had a clear view of the branding.

"Can you make out the brand?" Tee asked.

Jack took a moment to study the hip of the closest steer. "Looks like 8I," he said, after a moment.

"Makes a perfect fit over the ET brand," Tee observed.

"But there's more than the fifty head we've been track-ing," Jack said. "Where did the others come from?"

"We've been missing cattle before this, haven't we?" Tee asked.

"Yeah."

"Well, there's your answer."

"What're we gonna do?" Jack asked.

"Only one thing to do," Tee said. "Be suicide to tackle them by ourselves. We'll ease outta here, get our horses, and go get the others."

As they swung aboard their mounts, a rifle exploded and a bullet blasted the branch of a willow inches from Tee's head.

"Let's ride!" Tee yelled and slapped spurs to his mount. Jack followed so close behind, his mount nosed into the rear end of Tee's as bullets sprayed the brush.

"Get your rifles ready," Jenny ordered, hearing shots. "Don't hit Tee or Jack, but shoot to kill anyone chasing them."

Then Tee and Jack came into view, their horses stretched

flat with both riders down low over their saddle horns. A moment later, their pursuers came into view.

"Cut down on them!" Jenny yelled.

She focused in on a big rider in the lead. When he was near enough for her to catch a glimpse of his features, she lowered her rifle and stared, her face pale. "Ben Blount!" she whispered.

Two riders were knocked from their saddles before the outlaws turned and fled back into the canyon. When Jenny turned for a look at Tee, his saddle was empty. She gave a cry and ran to where Jack knelt beside the body of her friend and overseer.

Tee Martin was dead.

"Oh, Gosh!" she whispered. "They've killed this dear old man."

"Who, Miss Jenny?" Jack asked.

"Ben Blount! I saw him back there!"

"Ben Blount?" asked Jack. "Then we'll go after him. Come on, boys."

"No, Jack," Jenny said. "Let him go. The cattle aren't worth losing anyone else."

"But, Miss Jenny!" Jack replied.

"No," Jenny repeated. "We'll ride for the ranch. I don't want to see anyone else shot and killed," she continued. Her face reflected fierce determination, and Jack knew there was no use in arguing the point with her.

Chapter Twenty-six

Jason looked up from the garden where he was hoeing snap beans and recognized the rider's squat figure as Marshal Gruber. Dropping his hoe, he went to the house to wait for the marshal, wondering what Gruber might have on his mind to make such a long ride.

"Step down, Marshal. Care for some coffee?"

"Thanks, but I don't have the time," replied Gruber.

"Then what brings you out?"

"You lost any cattle recently?" the marshal asked.

"No."

"Wish I could say the same for your neighbors."

"You mean Jenny Taylor?"

"Yeah, and some others. She and her men chased the rustlers. Tee Martin was killed, and she turned back."

"Martin's dead?"

"Yeah. Jenny says she recognized Ben Blount among the bunch. Thought he was the leader. I'm rounding up a posse to go after them."

"When did this happen, Marshal?" Jason asked.

"Four days ago. They brought Tee back and buried him. Then Jack Crowe sent a rider in to notify me."

"Won't do no good to go after them, Marshal," Jason said. "That bunch drove those cattle into Mexico two days ago."

"We have to try. Will you be riding with us?"

"Don't think so, Marshal. Would if I thought there was a chance to catch up with them. Reckon I got a lot to do around here anyway."

"Your neighbors ain't gonna like this, Ward," the marshal said. "Just when everyone was beginning to forget the past and look on you as someone they could get along with."

When the marshal was gone, Jason called Mel and Stacy in from the range.

"I'm going after him," he said, after repeating what he'd learned.

"But you don't know where to start," Mel said.

"I'll find the place. Mel, saddle the sorrel for me and bring out a packhorse. Stacy, you fix up some grub. Pack ammunition and a couple of bags of water. I expect I'll be crossing some desert." He looked at his friend for a long moment. "I don't know when I'll be back. But the two of you can take care of things here."

"I think one of us should ride along, Jason," Mel said. "That's a mean bunch."

"No," Jason replied. "Blount will get rid of his men. He'll think they'll be a liability by drawing attention to him. And this is between him and me."

"Well, all right," Mel agreed reluctantly.

Jason knew there was little reason to push the sorrel, since he figured Blount had been on the move for at least two days. Instead, he took his time and rode to the Taylor place.

Jack Crowe saw him riding in and came from the barn.

"Afternoon, Ward," the foreman said. "What can we do for you?"

"You can tell me the location of the canyon where you found that stolen herd."

"You planning to ride after them?" Jack asked.

"Figured I might," Jason said, as he caught a glimpse of Jenny at a window.

"Wish I could go with you," Jack said, after he had finished giving directions to the canyon.

"Thanks anyway."

When Jason was finished talking with Jack, he stopped by the house and swung down. Jenny met him on the porch. "You did the right thing not fighting Blount," he told her.

"But you're going after him," she said.

"I got no choice, Jenny," he said. "He won't ever leave us alone. "You know that, don't you?"

"I guess, but be careful, Jason. He killed my father and he killed Tee. I think I'd die if anything happened to you."

"I'll be careful," he told her, and this time there was no hesitation. He took her in his arms and kissed her, though Jack stood nearby holding the sorrel.

Jenny stared after Jason until he had ridden out of sight. Then, turning, she went inside. *Dear God,* she prayed silently, *let him come back to me.*

The cattle trail leading south from the canyon was plainly visible, though it was a couple of days old. Jason followed it, sure now Blount was pushing the herd to Mexico. He followed the trail to the Rio Grande just north of Nogales, and left it there. Trailing the cattle into Nogales was impossible, but unless the herd had been sold at once, they would be somewhere among the corrals south of town. If he didn't find what he was looking for, he would hit some of the cantinas, spread a little silver around, and ask some discreet questions.

* * *

Jason covered more than half the pens before he found cattle. Some wore an 8I brand, but more than half still carried the Taylor brand.

A Mexican, obviously an official of the pens, approached him. "You interested to buy some cattle, Señor?" he asked.

"These cattle were stolen," Jason said.

"But I have a bill of sale, Señor," the Mexican said, taking a paper from his vest pocket and offering it to Jason. "You see the signature right there. Señor Ben Blount. I have bought many cattle from him over the years. There was never any trouble before."

"Ben Blount no longer owns the ET," Jason replied. "You buy any more cattle from him, you're a party to rustling, and I'll see that your neck is stretched." Jason's voice was quiet but hard as nails.

"No more, Señor," the man said. "I buy no more cattle from Señor Blount."

"Where did Blount go when you paid him?" Jason asked.

"He left here to visit the cantinas. That was day before yesterday. I doubt he is still there . . . Unless . . ." The Mexican did not finish his sentence.

"Unless what?"

"Unless he found his woman. If he did, he might still be here. He likes her very much."

"What's his woman's name and where does she live?" Jason asked, taking a gold piece from his pocket.

The man eyed the coin greedily. "Her name is Marlina, and she works at the *Chica* Cantina."

"Will you do one other thing for me?" Jason asked and held the coin out temptingly.

"Anything, Señor."

"Don't tell anyone I was here asking about Blount. If you do, I'll come back here and make you eat this coin."

"I tell no one, Señor," he said, and crossed himself.

Jason gave him the twenty-dollar gold piece.

The *Chica* Cantina was on the edge of town. Blount's big gray was tied to the hitch rack outside. Jason entered the cantina and then quickly stepped aside and waited for his eyes to adjust to the dark room.

Blount sat at a table with a young, dark-haired woman on his knee. As Jason watched, Blount gave the woman a pinch on her rear, laughingly loudly at her squeal of pain. With one arm still around the woman, he lifted a bottle of tequila to his mouth, intending to take a swig. He had the bottle halfway to his lips when he saw Jason. Dumping the woman from his lap, he scrambled up and clawed for his gun. The woman hit the floor on her rump and yelled something angrily in Spanish.

Blount got off the first shot, but he rushed it, his bullet striking the floor well in front of Jason. Jason took a step into the room, drew the Peacemaker, took careful aim, and fired. The bullet slammed into Blount, but the big man didn't go down. Staggering backward, he sank into the chair, managing to squeeze off another shot. His bullet struck the ceiling this time. He seemed to wilt suddenly, sliding out of the chair to the floor.

Jason walked to the front of the cantina and looked down at the lifeless body. He could hardly believe the long and violent struggle was over. Ben Blount would no longer pursue his evil plots against anyone else. As he looked at the dead man, Jason felt little elation, only satisfaction that he and Jenny would no longer have anything to fear from the man. Jason's only desire now was to head back to the valley and let Jenny and his friends know that he was all right and the long chase was over.

* * *

Two weeks later, Jason rode into the valley. He pulled up at the crest of the ridge and looked down. Cattle grazed along the stream and a few antelope fed among them. Kneeing the sorrel, he sent the horse toward the ranch house.

Stacy and Mel met him at the corral. "About time you got back," Mel said lightly, his satisfaction showing despite his effort to seem matter-of-fact in his welcome.

"About time," Mel added.

Jason shook their hands warmly. "Everything all right here?" he asked.

"Depends on how it strikes you, I guess," Mel replied.

"Don't talk in riddles," Jason demanded, suddenly uneasy. "Tell me what's wrong."

"Somebody's moved in on you," Stacy said.

Jason heard the front door to the adobe open. Turning, he saw Jenny come out.

"Oh, Jason!" she called.

They met halfway between the corral and the house.

"What are you doing here?" he asked.

"I sold my ranch and needed a place to stay," Jenny replied, smiling. "You think you could use a cook?"

"Under one condition," replied Jason.

"What condition?"

"You take the job for the rest of our lives."

"The job is filled," she said, and stepped into his arms.